"Galen Horvath, at your service."

Her skin was warm and lightly scented. Something sweet, with a hint of vanilla and some other slightly more heady spice. Whatever it was, his olfactory senses definitely appreciated it. A slight tremor of her hand made him release his hold on her.

Never one to be shy, his best girl piped up. "And I'm Ellie. Will you marry us?"

A smile tweaked the woman's lips. "Both of you? Now, there's a bargain," she said as her smile widened and made her eyes sparkle with obvious delight. "The answer is yes. I'm Peyton Earnshaw, and I would be delighted to marry you."

Galen watched her and felt something shift deep inside. That smile, her manner, her scent. It all coalesced into something powerful inside him. Lust, he told himself.

Pure physical attraction, that was all it was. And it was far, far more than he'd anticipated experiencing on meeting his bride.

* * *

Vengeful Vows is part of the Marriage at First Sight series from *USA TODAY* bestselling author Yvonne Lindsay.

Dear Reader,

As someone who met their life partner on a blind date, I have always loved the idea of matches being made for people. So, when I first dreamed up the Marriage at First Sight series, I had no idea how problematic it could be. We have couples who are destined to be together—on paper and by computer and through much analysis, they are each the other's perfect match. Simple. Or so I thought.

In *Vengeful Vows*, Peyton Earnshaw is a successful features journalist with a difficult past and revenge on her mind. Galen Horvath, CEO of Horvath Hotels and Resorts, is a knight in shining armor whose focus is on protecting his family and the future security of his new ward at all costs. When they clash, they clash spectacularly, especially when the object of Peyton's revenge, Galen's grandmother, is revealed to him.

I do hope you enjoy this installment in my series and, if you haven't already, do check out the previous two books, *Tangled Vows* and *Inconveniently Wed*. I love to hear from my readers—contact links are on my website, yvonnelindsay.com.

Best wishes and happy reading!

Yvonne Lindsay

YVONNE LINDSAY

VENGEFUL VOWS

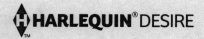

Recycling programs
for this product may
not exist in your area.

ISBN-13: 978-1-335-60360-9

Vengeful Vows

www.Harlequin.com

Printed in U.S.A.

Award-winning *USA TODAY* bestselling author **Yvonne Lindsay** has always preferred the stories in her head to the real world. Married to her blind-date sweetheart and with two adult children, she spends her days crafting the stories of her heart. In her spare time she can be found with her nose firmly in someone else's book.

Books by Yvonne Lindsay

Harlequin Desire

Wed at Any Price

Honor-Bound Groom
Stand-In Bride's Seduction
For the Sake of the Secret Child

Courtesan Brides

Arranged Marriage, Bedroom Secrets
Contract Wedding, Expectant Bride

Marriage at First Sight

Tangled Vows
Inconveniently Wed
Vengeful Vows

Visit her Author Profile page at Harlequin.com, or yvonnelindsay.com, for more titles.

To my blind-date hero,
thank you for all your years of support
and encouragement.

One

Alice Horvath—matriarch of the Horvath family, former CEO of Horvath Corporation and creator of Match Made in Marriage—surveyed the candlelit, flower-bedecked room and tried to ignore the trepidation that filled her. She didn't know why she was so nervous about the union of her third-eldest grandson, Galen, to a woman who was so perfect for him it had actually brought tears to her eyes when she'd made the match. But for some reason, despite all her usual attention to detail, she felt as though she didn't have quite her usual grip on what would happen next.

Their future happiness was her only goal, but for once she couldn't see that far ahead for them as clearly as she did with the others. If they made it, it would require hard work and commitment from them both.

Had she taken an unnecessary risk? Galen had said he didn't want a grand passion, but everyone deserved that, didn't they?

She thought of her late husband, Eduard, and to-night missed him more keenly than she had in a long time. But she wasn't ready to rest in peace with him yet. She still had too much work to do, and the success of this marriage was a part of that, no matter what secrets it brought out of the woodwork.

Galen closed his eyes briefly then started as he felt a small hand take his and give it a squeeze.

"It'll be okay," Ellie whispered. "She's going to love you."

He squeezed back gently. "She's going to love *us*," he affirmed.

He flicked an imaginary piece of lint from his suit sleeve and looked sideways at his best girl. Ellie grinned back up at him, and Galen felt his heart swell. Both his brother, Valentin, and his cousin Ilya had offered to stand here at the altar with him but this wasn't about a traditional marriage. This was about providing security for nine-year-old Ellie, so it made sense that she stand up with him as he married a total stranger. Poor kid; she deserved so much better than him, but he was doing his best by her, and would con-tinue to do so for the rest of his life.

When he'd assumed guardianship of Ellie after her parents' shocking and sudden deaths in a car crash just over three months ago, his life as he'd known it had come to a screaming halt. No more wild parties.

No more playboy lifestyle. All the commitment he'd dodged for most of his adult life had come to him in one complete package. He hadn't been ready for it, but then neither had his best friends, Ellie's mom and dad, expected to die, either.

He cast one more look around the room, ensuring everything was as it should be. He wouldn't be the CEO of Horvath Hotels and Resorts without triple-checking everything all the time. He knew how to keep people happy—all kinds of people. Surely, that would help when it came to keeping his new wife happy, too?

"She's here!" Ellie whispered hoarsely. "And she's so pretty."

Galen looked to the door at the end of the carpeted aisle in the function room and, honest to God, felt his breath catch in his lungs. Pretty? No, that didn't even begin to describe the woman paused there at the end. Her face was a picture of serenity, her head poised on a long, graceful neck. Her hair was pulled back in a loose updo that made his fingers itch to extract each and every pin and let her hair fall down over the slender bare shoulders exposed by her strapless gown. Her skin glowed. A diamond drop necklace sat low on her décolletage, drawing his eyes to the rapid rise and fall of her chest—to the hint of the soft swell of her breasts, framed by the gown's neckline. His gaze drifted lower, to the tiny waist cinched in a satin sash with a cluster of silk and diamanté flowers and then to the three tiers of flowing shimmering fabric that spread like a cloud around her.

"She looks like a princess," Ellie said, loudly this time so that everyone in the room turned their heads and a collective gasp of awe filtered through the air.

"Let's make her our queen, shall we?" Galen said and, still holding Ellie's hand, he walked toward his bride.

As they drew closer, he noticed the flickering pulse in her neck. So perhaps she wasn't quite as serene as she projected. That was fine by him. In a way, he'd have felt some reserve about marrying someone who *wasn't* just a little rattled at the prospect of meeting their future life partner for the first time at the altar. And while he'd seen his brother and his cousin make successful matches that way, he'd never for a moment considered it for himself. Truth be told, he'd never even considered marriage before Ellie.

The woman's eyes flared slightly, her bluish-gray irises almost consumed by her pupils in the candle-light.

"My groom, I presume?" she said in a voice that was a tiny bit husky and a whole lot of nervous.

"Galen Horvath, at your service," he said, taking her free hand and lifting it to his lips.

Her skin was warm and lightly scented. Something sweet, with a hint of vanilla and a slightly headier spice. A slight tremor of her hand made him release his hold.

Never one to be shy, his best girl piped up. "And I'm Ellie. Will you marry us?"

A smile tweaked the woman's lips. "Both of you? Now, there's a bargain," she said as her smile widened and her eyes sparkled with obvious delight. "The answer is yes. I'm Peyton Earnshaw, and I would be delighted to marry you."

Galen felt something shift deep inside as he watched her. Her smile, her manner, her scent. It all coalesced into something powerful inside him. Lust, he told himself. Pure physical attraction; that was all it was. And it was far, far more than he'd anticipated experiencing on meeting his bride. The tension that had gripped him all day began to ease. This was going to be okay. *They* were going to be okay, he corrected himself.

Peyton had done a lot of things in the pursuit of investigative journalism, but she'd never gotten married before. When she'd decided to do an exposé on Alice Horvath she'd been delighted to discover an old college acquaintance among Alice's staff. And when she'd learned the matriarch's own grandson was searching for a bride, she'd called in an old debt and secured Michelle's assistance gaming the system to match Peyton's profile with the grandson's. The fact that the matchmaking results could be manipulated like that lent weight to Peyton's argument that Alice Horvath's company was a complete fraud in the first place.

Peyton swallowed her nerves as, flanked by Galen Horvath and Ellie, she walked down the aisle toward the celebrant, who waited with a benevolent smile. She'd been prepared to do anything to achieve her goal—even marry a stranger—and now here she was.

Acutely aware of the warm strength of Galen's

hand holding hers, she tried to calm the unaccustomed racing of her heart. He was just a man. Seriously, her groom could have been anyone—but he
wasn't. He was one of Alice Horvath's many grand-
children. He could have been short, tall, thin, full fig-
ured, hirsute. He was tall, more handsome than any
star she'd seen at the movies lately, and he exuded a
charisma that she felt pulling on her in ways she'd
never expected. And his touch was doing weird things
to her insides. Things that she prided herself on not
feeling. Things she'd inured herself to—by choice.
She wasn't some naive creature full of unrealistic expectations. Oh sure, she knew you could fall in love,
but she also knew the pain of a stupid decision made
in the heat of the moment, and she wasn't going to
make that kind of mistake ever again.

"Everything okay?"

A soft whisper of breath caressed her ear as Galen
leaned close to her.

"Just peachy," she said with a bright smile that she
was far from feeling.

His eyes met hers and he stared at her a moment
before his face broke into a smile that literally stole
the breath from her lungs. He gave her hand a gentle
squeeze before letting go. She was going to have to be
careful around this guy, she told herself as she composed her features and faced the celebrant.

The service was simple. She'd have liked to have
said it was honest but she was here under false pre-
tenses. It gave her a moment's pause when she considered that what she planned to do would not only

affect the man she was marrying, but also the little girl, who looked up at him with trust and adoration. Well, she just wouldn't let anyone, herself included, become too attached; that was all there was to it. And when her in-depth article exposing Alice Horvath for the manipulative and cruel woman she truly was hit the newsstands, no one would be hurt but the woman who'd destroyed Peyton's father and, in turn, her entire family. Even the baby she'd been forced to give away.

Peyton blinked back the sudden burn in her eyes. Show no weakness. That had been her mantra then and it remained her mantra now.

"Congratulations!" the celebrant announced with warmth and enthusiasm—as if this was a real wedding and as if they were planning a real future together. "I now pronounce you husband and wife. You may kiss the bride."

Oh, no.

Peyton froze as Galen took both her hands in his and leaned toward her. A sense of inevitability seeped through to her bones as she instinctively closed the final gap between them and allowed his lips to brush hers. Except it was more than a brush—it was an enticement. The gentle press of his mouth against hers sent her pulse thudding out of control, and when she parted her lips—to protest, she would tell herself later—he took advantage and tasted her with a practiced sweep of his tongue. She should have pulled back, she should have ended it, but she didn't. Instead, like some sappy lovestruck teenager, she leaned even closer and kissed him back as if this was a real marriage and they'd been anticipating this moment for months.

When he withdrew she felt oddly bereft, even shaken. She looked up at him and saw the same kind of expression reflected back at her and instantly knew keeping Galen Horvath—her *husband*—at arm's length was going to prove a great deal more challenging than she'd hoped.

"Yay, we're a family!" Ellie said excitedly as she wrapped her skinny little arms around them both and gave them a big squeeze. "Nothing bad can happen now."

"Nothing ba—" Peyton started.

"I'll explain more later. Right now we have some celebrating to do."

And they did. They took photos with their guests, including a few of her friends from college she'd kept in touch with. The Horvaths had been suitably sympathetic when she'd explained that her mother had died when she was a child and her father was unable to make it for the wedding.

After they were done with the formal photos, they toasted and ate and danced and toasted some more. And with every step perfectly in tune with her new partner, Peyton kept a smile on her face and acted as if this was exactly what she'd wanted all her life.

When the lights dimmed in the reception room and the music slowed to a dreamy romantic number, Galen took her back into his arms and led her out onto the dance floor.

"Don't you ever get tired?" Peyton teased. "You haven't been allowed to sit down yet."

He flashed a brief grin at her before his expression grew more serious. "I wanted to let you know what was behind Ellie's statement earlier."

"Do tell," she encouraged when Galen fell silent.

If she wasn't mistaken, a shimmer of moisture appeared in his eyes. He tilted his head back slightly and blinked hard before meeting her gaze again. Then he drew a deep breath and his words came in a rush.

"Ellie's my ward. Her parents died in a car crash at the beginning of the year. They were my best friends."

Galen's voice cracked and Peyton was instantly flooded with compassion. She knew what it felt like to have your world ripped apart unexpectedly. But to lose both parents at the same time? That was almost too awful to contemplate. She waited, not wanting to fill the new silence between them with platitudes.

After a couple of minutes he continued. "I think she's done really well coping with her loss. Often, she's coped better than me. She's had grief counseling and we haven't made any changes to her lifestyle that she wasn't ready to make. In fact, it was her idea I buy a house in her old neighborhood for us both to live in. She said being at her old family home made her too sad."

"So you did that?"

"Well, it's a work in progress. For now we're staying here in my apartment at the hotel. I hope you can help us choose our home together."

"Our home together. Right. That's a big thing to ask when we've only just met, don't you think?"

He nodded. "True, but if we're going to make our marriage work properly, we need to be living under the same roof, right?" When she didn't answer, he continued. "Anyway, I thought Ellie and I were doing okay but she blindsided me one day. I found her crying in her room and when I managed to get to the root of the problem it floored me. It wasn't something I could just throw money at, or tease a smile out of, or distract away."

"What was it?" she prompted.

"She told me she was terrified about what would happen if I died like her mom and dad. If one day she was completely alone." He drew in a deep breath and looked around the room at the revelers. His voice was low and intense when he spoke again. "I knew then that I needed to get married, to find a wife who wanted to share Ellie's life with me. To help her feel secure and loved and needed, the way her parents did. I want to be totally honest with you, Peyton. This marriage didn't start out in a traditional sense, but I'd like to think we can work together to achieve that eventually. We've both come to Match Made in Marriage with the same goal. Finding a life partner. I'm being clear and up-front about my reasons for needing to find a wife. Right now Ellie is the most important person in my world, and I will do whatever I can to make her happy. I need to know you'll commit to that, too."

Two

Peyton didn't know where to look or what to think. She was consumed by guilt. Suddenly, this assignment was skewing out of her control. Not only did she feel like she was constantly fighting with her instincts to just let go and enjoy being with the man who held her so capably in his arms as they did another turn around the dance floor. This also wasn't what she'd signed up for. She'd expected an uncomplicated union, a chance to dig for more dirt on Alice Horvath and eventually the opportunity to extract from her the apology her father and her late mother had been due for far too long.

And now what? Now she was married; that was what. It wasn't the wedding she'd dreamed of as a child, where her father would proudly walk her down the aisle, but one engineered by a stranger so she could marry a stranger. She had been confident she could handle it. How hard could it be?

But now she was a stepmom, too. And not just a stepmom, but to a child who already knew far too much about loss and how the whole world could be upended in the blink of an eye. Already Peyton felt a pull toward the girl—how could she not? Ellie was bright and engaging and demonstrative. Everything she herself had been at that age. Except when Peyton's world had turned upside down she'd retreated into herself. She'd been nothing like Ellie. Did she dare risk crushing Ellie's spirit? Could Peyton enter into this debacle of a marriage and then exit it without causing harm? It was doubtful. And she was in, whether she liked it or not, for at least the next three months under the terms of the agreement she'd signed only a few weeks ago. Signed, secure in the belief that this would be a simple matter of going through the experience, writing her story and leaving without looking back.

Galen watched her, obviously expecting some kind of answer. He'd been open with her about his expectations and it was only fair that he expected openness in return. But honesty was something she couldn't give him, even if she wanted to. Her entire adult life she'd been gearing up for this moment. To exact the revenge for Alice's unfounded accusations against her dad of improper record keeping and misappropriation of funds. Accusations that had cast a permanent pall on his professional career and made him untrustworthy in the eyes of every potential new employer. Accusations that had put additional strain on her mother's diminishing health—she'd developed complications from her multiple sclerosis—which had subsequently drained what little they had in the bank and left them living on handouts and whatever sporadic income her father could earn. They'd been unable to pay medical bills for treatment that might have eased her mother's condition and had ended up having to move from California to Oregon, where the cost of living was lower, but which put her mom even farther from the medical team who'd overseen her care.

A little of the anger that had driven Peyton all these years sparked back to life, blanketing the guilt so there was little more than a pang left.

"I committed to marrying you, Galen. I will do my part."

He tensed as if waiting to hear more, but she wasn't prepared to outright lie and make false declarations. She was here to do a job and to close a chapter in her and her family's life. And then there was the other reason. The reason she barely allowed herself to think of. The child she'd been forced to give away. Had her family's circumstances been different, she would have been able to keep her. Circumstances she could lay fully and completely at the feet of the woman walking toward them right now. With no money left in her college fund, Peyton had had to take out student loans to go to college. No matter how carefully she'd crunched the numbers there was no way she could afford food, rent, utilities and childcare on top of her loan repayments and her parents had had no way to help physically, emotionally or financially. After all these years, and all her painstaking planning, it was coming to fruition now. She couldn't afford to take her eye off her goal, for anyone.

"I guess that's all I can ask," he said. "And look, here's Nagy to check on her new chick."

"Nagy?" Peyton asked, quietly bristling at the idea of being one of Alice Horvath's *anything*.

"It's Hungarian. A diminutive of *nagymama*, for 'grandmother.'"

And then Alice was upon them. Though she was slightly built and petite, there was a steeliness to her gaze, and her back was ramrod straight. It was clear this woman didn't suffer fools gladly; Peyton could tell the woman who'd controlled the Horvath Corporation at its head office in California for many years after her husband's death was formidable. But as Alice drew nearer, a smile appeared on the old woman's face. It softened her and made her look entirely approachable. This wasn't the face of the monster Peyton had always believed her to be.

Galen's arm tightened around her waist and she involuntarily nestled closer. She had to look and act the part of newlywed, no matter what. And it wasn't so difficult, was it? He was hardly unattractive and the lean, hard lines of his body beneath his suit felt uncommonly right against her, confusing her even more.

"Congratulations, you two," Alice said warmly as she reached up and kissed Galen on the cheek then took Peyton's hands in hers. "You look wonderful together. I'm sure you'll be very happy."

Peyton smiled, or was it a snarl with her nemesis standing right in front of her? She couldn't be entirely sure. "Thank you," she managed, her voice sounding stiff and unnatural.

"We're a bit overwhelming en masse, aren't we?" Alice said with a conspiratorial smile. "But you'll get used to us. Everyone does."

By decree of Alice Horvath, Peyton thought bitterly. Get used to them and play by their rules, or get out. She forced herself to hold that smile on her face and took in a deep breath of relief when Alice let go of her hands and turned once again to her grandson. Peyton watched, intrigued by the genuine affection between them. There was nothing stilted or fake about the fondness they showed one another. She let their conversation wash over her and surveyed the rest of the room. It almost looked like the celebration of a real wedding as people laughed and danced and ate and drank. And yet she felt completely separate from all of it. Had she bitten off more than she could chew by taking this assignment?

Galen sensed his new bride's disengagement and hastened to end the conversation with his grandmother. It was important to him that Peyton feel she'd made the right decision. He was very good at making other people feel good—about their choices, about themselves, about him. He aimed to please, always, and it had stood him in good stead with his career choice and drew a lot of people to him. But he had the distinct impression that Peyton was not going to be an easy sell. He wouldn't be able to simply waltz her off into this new happily-ever-after life. There was a reserve about her, even though she was going through all the motions and smiling in all the right places. And he was determined to break that wall down, brick by brick if he had to.

He stroked the curve of her waist but her body remained rigid. Maybe his touch was too much, too soon. He told himself to let her go but the thought of doing so held no appeal at all. He was genuinely attracted to her and mentally gave his grandmother a thumbs-up for their pairing. And he'd have bet that Peyton was attracted to him, too, though she was doing her best not to show it. As soon as this party was over, things would be different. They could all relax. He thought about the Horvath resort in Hawaii where they'd be heading by private jet tonight. Hopefully there, soothed by the balmy breeze and the lush beauty of the landscape, Peyton would unwind a little more and allow him to get to know her better.

"Nagy, could you give Peyton and I a little time alone? We'll need to get ready to leave soon. Perhaps you could mind Ellie for me and we can collect her before we head to the airport?"

"Of course. It would be my pleasure. Ellie is such a delight. When you're back from honeymoon, I'd love it if she could stay with me in Ojai for a weekend."

His grandmother gave Peyton and him both a kiss on the cheek and went off in search of the nine-year-old.

"Ellie is coming with us?" Peyton asked with a surprised expression on her face.

"I hope that's okay. She's on spring break right now, so it made sense to me to include her and, as we weren't permitted contact between one another before the wedding, I couldn't exactly ask you."

"No, it's not a problem at all," Peyton answered, looking more than a little relieved.

Was it because she wouldn't be left alone with him, that they'd have Ellie as a buffer between them? Galen gave an internal shrug. Whatever; it didn't matter as long as this worked out. Ellie already liked his new bride. She was a bright kid and knowing she liked Peyton was half the battle won. If they could cement that into something strong and lasting—a family unit that would make her feel loved and secure for the rest of her childhood—then he would have succeeded in fulfilling the promise he'd made to his two dead friends as they were laid to rest. Failure was not an option.

"Are you curious about where we're going?"

"I'm assuming it's somewhere warm. I was told to pack light clothing and swimwear."

"It's perpetually warm. We're off to a Horvath resort a little over two and a half thousand miles east-southeast of here," he teased.

"That would be your resort on Maui, right?"

"You've been doing your research on us," he answered, surprised at her very specific response.

Her cheeks colored. "Research? What makes you think that?"

She sounded defensive. Definitely not what he'd

been hoping for just before they left to change for travel.

"Let's just say I'm not used to people being as well-informed about my business as you apparently are," he said, attempting to soothe her.

"Information is my business," she said smoothly, her demeanor relaxing slightly.

"And your business is?"

"I'm a reporter, freelance."

"A travel reporter? We've been featured in quite a few magazines and blogs. Maybe you've been our guest before?"

She shook her head. "No, not travel. Didn't you say we needed to go and change?"

Her subject switch was about as subtle as dropping an old typewriter from the top of a tall building onto the pavement below. But he wasn't slow to take a hint and he had plenty of time to get to know her better.

"We do. A chopper is taking us to SeaTac in about an hour."

"It doesn't take me an hour to get ready," Peyton answered with a gurgle of laughter. "Do I look that high-maintenance?"

Her laugh was intoxicating, the first sign of unfettered emotion he'd seen in her so far. He knew he wanted more of it, more of her being natural, being herself.

"Well, we might be able to go earlier, provided we can say goodbye to our guests without too many hold-ups. It won't change our departure time from SeaTac, though—the flight plan has already been filed. We're taking one of our company jets."

"How the other half lives, huh?" she said, softening her words with a smile.

"You're a part of that now. Flight time is about six hours once we're wheels up."

"How late will it be when we arrive?"

"Hawaii's three hours behind us, so, all going smoothly, about seven p.m."

"It's going to be a long day for Ellie."

"She'll be okay. She was used to traveling with her parents and can sleep on the flight if she wants to. You can, too."

She shook her head. "Sadly, I'm one of those who can never sleep on a plane."

"Always vigilant?"

"Something like that. Well, I guess we'd better get on our way, then?"

"Let me see you up to your room," he said, taking her arm. "Did you want to throw your bouquet first?"

She shrugged. "Sure."

"Give me a minute to get it organized."

"I'll go get the bouquet."

He watched as she glided across the room toward the main table where she'd left her flowers. The gentle sway of her hips totally mesmerized him.

"Nice wife," his brother, Valentin, said as he approached.

"It's a good thing you have your own, or I'd be making you keep your eyes off mine."

"And I wouldn't trade her for the world."

Galen heard the intense emotion in Valentin's words. He and Imogene had been married once before, and until Nagy had reunited them in a Match Made in Marriage wedding, they'd both been unhappy. Now they were together again, for good this time, and Galen felt a glimmer of envy—wishing he, too, could experience the kind of relationship they had. But his bed had been made for him when he'd agreed to be Ellie's guardian and then signed up to find a wife so Ellie could feel safe again. He wasn't expecting romance and roses. What he needed for his best girl was stability, and hopefully, he could achieve that with Peyton.

"Peyton's going to toss her bouquet soon. I need to let the emcee know so he can make the announcement."

"Watch out for the stampede of cousins." Valentin laughed, but then his expression grew serious. "Galen, I just wanted to say a few private words."

"And they are?"

"We only get one shot at life, so we need to make the most of every minute. You're going to hit some roadblocks in this marriage, that's a given, but you need to be prepared to work through every one of them."

"I'm not afraid of hard work. You know that."

"Yeah, I know. I wish you a lifetime of happiness."

Valentin wrapped his arms around him in a fierce hug and Galen gave him back as good as he got. "Thanks, Val," he said, his voice suddenly thick with emotion. "I'm going to do my best."

"You're going to need to. Marrying someone you

already know and love isn't always easy, but marrying a stranger..."

Galen looked across the room to where Peyton had been corralled by some of his aunties. "Yeah, but what a stranger, right?"

His brother slapped him on the back with another laugh then left him to find the emcee.

Valentin hadn't been wrong about the stampede. All their female cousins together with several women he'd never met before tonight, mostly Peyton's guests, jostled for the moment she released the bouquet. The scramble was both undignified and highly amusing, but Galen was shocked when he saw his nerdy IT expert cousin, Sophia, emerge triumphant at the end. He took advantage of the ensuing chaos to take Peyton by the hand and, calling out a good-night to everyone, lead her away.

"Ellie knows we're coming back for her, right?" Peyton looked worried.

Galen was touched at her concern for a child she'd only just met. "Of course. Her suitcase is already in the chopper. She knows I won't leave her behind. Ilya, my cousin, and his wife, Yasmin, will bring her to the helipad just before we're due to depart. For now she can party it up a little with my younger cousins."

"You do have a big family," Peyton commented.

"Yeah, I do. And you? Brothers? Sisters?"

She shook her head. "Just me...and my dad," she added.

"He couldn't come today?"

Her lips firmed into a straight line. "It's difficult—we barely talk. I'd rather not discuss it."

He wanted to press for more details, but one look at her face made him file that away for another time. Bit by bit, he was learning there were going to be a hell of a lot of layers to peel through to get to the core of what made up his new wife. It was probably a good thing that he was a patient man.

Three

Peyton pushed her hair off her face for the hundredth time. The onshore breeze delighted in tangling her hair at every opportunity, but it wasn't all bad. At least the wind was warm and gentle, not damp and biting cold like it so often was back home in Washington. After their arrival last night she'd been bone weary and had barely paid any attention to their luxurious surroundings. She didn't know what she'd expected exactly, when Galen had said they'd be honeymooning at a Horvath resort, but this certainly hadn't been it. It wasn't a hotel, although there apparently was one here somewhere in the many sprawling acres of the complex, but a large and airy house that faced the water and was full of dazzling sunshine. She'd been relieved to discover they each had their own bedroom, too, along with their own private beach, where Ellie was busy digging holes and creating roads and moats and tunnels, and squealing happily at the rising tide as it demolished her hard work.

"Can I braid your hair for you?" Galen asked from the sun lounger beside her.

"You?" Peyton was surprised by the offer.

"I'll have you know I've become quite adept at styling long hair. I don't even have to use a vacuum cleaner hose to get Ellie's ponytail perfect anymore."

"A what?"

"Check it out online. I tell you, YouTube is king when it comes to learning new skills."

She couldn't help but laugh at the idea of Galen even knowing how to use a vacuum cleaner, let alone having the skills to use a vacuum cleaner to tie Ellie's hair in a ponytail. But she was always up for a challenge and, heck, let's face it, she was curious to see how he proposed to tame her tangled locks.

"Okay, then. Show me your talents," Peyton said, sitting up on her lounger and turning her back to him.

"Now, there's an invitation I don't get every day," he said, his voice dropping an octave.

She couldn't help it; her body reacted with a shimmer of desire. She had no words to describe it, this stupid reaction to a tone of voice, but suddenly she was hyperaware of the man as he moved closer behind her. She dug into her beach bag for her hairbrush.

"You might want to use this first," she said, passing it back to him. "There's a hair tie on the handle, too."

He took the hairbrush, and the next moment his

fingers were working their way through her hair, touching her scalp and skimming the back of her neck as he eased the hairbrush through the knots. She'd never in her life believed that having her hair brushed by a stranger could feel erotic. But there was something deeply sensual about the way Galen followed each stroke of the brush with the touch of his fingers on her scalp. It made her want to sigh with pleasure.

When he was done, she was on the verge of becoming putty in his hands. She felt a moment's relief that she was facing away from him so he couldn't see the way her nipples had become taut peaks against the thin fabric of her one-piece swimsuit in response to this most innocent of touches. But then he started to run his fingers through her hair again and every muscle in her body clenched.

"You okay? I'm not hurting you, am I?" Galen asked.

He was so close she felt his breath on her shoulder and shivered a little.

"I'm fine," she said in a voice that was tight with control.

He was simply doing her hair, for goodness' sake. Not seducing her. How this normal, everyday act could be playing such havoc with her senses was beyond her but she needed to get herself under control. She focused her gaze on Ellie and for a moment envied her the freedom of not caring who she was or what she looked like or what hurts had been visited upon her. Instead, she could just be carefree and in the moment. Industrious one minute, lying flat out on the sand the next, then laughing as she got to her feet and plunged into the water to wash off the sand five seconds later.

Galen began sectioning her hair.

"Do you want under or over?" he asked.

"I beg your pardon?"

"Your braid. Under, so it sits flat, or over, so it sits on top?"

"I never knew there was a difference."

"Your mom never did this for you?"

"My mom was sick for a long time, and my dad, well, let's just say he didn't have the benefit of online videos when I was growing up."

She swallowed against the surprising wave of emotion that choked her. There'd been days when her mom could meet her at the front door of their rented home with a smile and then there'd been others when she couldn't even raise a hand to wipe a tear from her cheek. The disease that had plagued her had taken its toll on everyone, and the fiercely guarded memories of those times always shook Peyton to the core.

"Anyway, does it matter?" she said a little more sharply than she'd intended.

"Over it is. And tomorrow we can go into the intricacies of the herringbone braid. Now, be still. I need to concentrate on this."

He fell silent as he worked. When it was over, he rested his hands on top of her shoulders. His palms were warm and his fingers gentle, but to her they felt like brands on her bare skin.

"Admiring your handiwork?" she asked with a note of sarcasm.

"Something like that. Did you know that you have these really soft curls of baby hair that grow at the nape of your neck?"

She shivered as he touched them, winding one around a finger. His knuckle brushed the back of her neck, sending her body into sensation overload. Who knew the back of her neck was so sensitive? Then her whole body went into shock as she felt the imprint of his lips right there at her nape. She bolted up from her lounger in an instinctive attempt to create more distance between them and adjusted her sunglasses on her face as she turned around and looked down on him.

Galen looked up at her unashamedly. "Sorry, couldn't help myself."

He flashed her another of those devil-may-care grins and rose from his lounger before jogging along the beach to where Ellie was fashioning a turtle sand sculpture. Peyton watched him join his ward with an enthusiasm she envied. Even in the short time she'd begun to get to know him, she recognized he had a knack for making everything look so uncomplicated. No doubt he was the life and soul of every party he attended, she thought with a touch of venom. The charmed billionaire who never had a care in his privileged world. He'd never had to come from school to a quiet house and wonder if today would be the day that he'd discover his mom dead in her bed. Or that the next knock on the door was from the sheriff to evict them from another home.

And then again, he'd known loss, she reminded herself with an effort to be fair. Ellie's parents' deaths had obviously affected him, and her research had uncovered he'd lost his own father when he was in his early teens. That must have been hard. Maybe his carefree act was just that. An act. She shrugged, picked up her sarong and knotted it at her hip before pushing her feet into a pair of crystal-studded thongs and walking along the beach to supervise the sculpting. Whether it was an act or not, it didn't matter to her because she wasn't here to enjoy Galen Horvath's company. She was here to do a job and she needed to remember that.

It was midnight, and Galen was mentally worn out and physically uncomfortable. There ought to be a law against suits and ties in tropical climates, he thought as he unknotted his tie and entered the villa that was home for the duration of their honeymoon.

"Good of you to come back." An acerbic voice came from the depths of the overstuffed couch facing the moonlit water. "I was beginning to wonder if you'd left us for good."

"Did you miss me?" Galen said, refusing to rise to Peyton's bait.

The woman had been so intent on keeping her distance from him that he'd almost begun to wonder if she'd even miss him when he had to work. Of course, working on honeymoon was not ideal, but the resort was on the verge of signing an agreement for a major expansion with an overseas partner, and certain things needed to be dealt with right here, right now.

"Ellie missed you," Peyton said, rising from the couch and facing him with her hands on her hips.

Galen's throat went dry as he took her in. She was silhouetted in the light behind her, exposing the slim, lean lines of her body beneath the sheer cream on the lemon-patterned sundress she wore. He'd seen her in her swimsuit and, yes, she was incredible to look at. But like this? She was mystery and mayhem all in one package. The sharp sound of her voice dragged him into reality.

"I was beginning to wonder if you'd married me just so you could have a babysitter. I have to say, if that's your parenting style, I feel sorry for Ellie because she deserves better than that."

Deserved better than him, too, perhaps? Galen felt his anger rise but, as ever, he pushed a lid down firmly on it and deflected her words with a smile. "Ellie knew I would be tied up all day."

"It doesn't mean she didn't miss you. She gets really anxious when you're not around. Did you know that?"

A shaft of guilt struck him in the chest. The last thing on earth he ever wanted to do was cause Ellie any distress. "What do you mean exactly?"

"She sounded tense at dinnertime, asking when you'd be back. I tried to distract her. Let her beat me at cards."

"Let her?" He cocked a half grin. The kid was a demon at cards.

"Okay, so she thrashed me. But when you weren't home by bedtime she got really upset. She was terrified something had happened to you, no matter what I said."

Galen nodded, accepting that he should have reached out to let her know he wouldn't be home until very late. Even though she'd been in his care for several months now, he was still adjusting to the responsibility. But they'd already been here on Maui for three days and Ellie had seemed equally happy to be with Peyton as with him—he'd been certain she'd be okay. Clearly, he'd been wrong.

"I'm sorry. I'll talk to her about it tomorrow."

"Would that be before or after your next business meeting?"

A kernel of warmth sparked to life deep inside him. Peyton might be angry at him but she was very firmly in Ellie's corner and that was what he'd hoped for all along—that he'd marry a woman who'd be comfortable in a maternal role with Ellie.

"There won't be any more business meetings. I promise. Not while we're on honeymoon, anyway."

"Until the next emergency arises and you need to offload your responsibilities again?"

He fought to keep his features neutral as he replied. "I don't make a habit of offloading anything. I'm sorry if caring for Ellie was such a burden to you."

Color flamed in her cheeks and her eyes grew bright. She looked like she was about to light off like a firecracker. Before she could respond, he put up a hand.

"Look, I'm sorry—that was uncalled for. I shouldn't have assumed that you'd look after Ellie when I couldn't."

"You don't even know me," Peyton said, a grimace twisting her beautiful face.

Galen walked closer to her and took one of her hands. "You're right. I don't know you, yet. I do, however, know you're trustworthy. We wouldn't have been matched if you weren't."

Peyton nodded ever so slightly. "She was upset tonight, Galen. I hated it."

Compassion flooded him and he squeezed her hand gently. "You feel so helpless, don't you?"

The anger that had been holding her rigid dropped out of her just like that.

"Yes, and I didn't like it. I'm sorry I took it out on you. But don't think I'm letting you off the hook."

"I know, and I'll make it up to both of you. I am a man of my word, Peyton. No more business on this vacation."

"Thank you."

She pulled her hand free and started to gather up her things, including some handwritten notes and a laptop computer.

"You were working?" he asked.

"Not until Ellie went to bed, which was only a couple of hours ago because she was so upset."

"I didn't mean it like that—no need to be defensive."

She raised her brows at him.

"I didn't. I'm merely interested. Is this a new article you're working on?"

"I don't discuss my work until it's published."

Peyton hugged her things to her as if hiding them from his gaze. Fair enough, but she was making it very difficult for them to find common ground for discussion and to get to know one another. So far both family and her work were off-limits. So what did that leave them? Not a lot.

"I can respect that. Your work is sensitive, then?"

"Usually, and this is particularly so. I'm not being obstructive. It's just the way I work. Okay?"

"Like I said, no problem. Hey, would you like to put your things away where my prying eyes can't see them and come and join me on the patio for a nightcap?"

She hesitated. He was beginning to brace himself for a flat no, when she nodded and said she'd be right back. Galen shrugged out of his jacket and yanked the tail of his tie through his collar. Valentin had been right. This marriage thing wasn't easy, especially when you were married to a stranger.

The other day, brushing her hair, he'd felt as though they'd reached a new level of closeness. But apparently going to work today had thrown all of that out the window and he was back to square one. He had to make this work, for Ellie. He felt a pang of guilt as he threw his things on a chair and went down the hallway toward Ellie's bedroom.

Since her parents' accident she'd been sleeping with a night-light and her door slightly ajar. He entered her room and settled gently on the edge of her bed. Ellie's eyes flashed wide open in an instant.

"You're home!" She sat bolt upright and her little arms wrapped around his neck.

His heart squeezed tight and he hugged her back. "Yeah, I'm home, so no more worrying, okay? I thought we had a deal. You're supposed to talk to me about the things that make you feel upset."

"I know," she said softly as she pulled away. "It's just hard when you're not here."

"I'm sorry I was gone so long today. It won't happen again while we're on vacation, I promise, but it will probably happen again when we're home. But I promise you this, too. I'll make sure you're never alone and you can always get whoever is with you to text me at any time."

"Even when you're in an important meeting?"

"Even then. Nothing and no one is more important to me than you, Ellie. I'm here for you. Always."

"Okay," she said on a yawn.

"Now, back to sleep, young lady. Tomorrow is a new day."

"Thanks, Galen. I love you."

"I love you, too, kiddo."

Galen pressed one more kiss to her forehead and then rose from the bed. She was already asleep by the time he got to the door. He looked back on her, his heart so full of love for this little girl it sometimes took his breath away. Moments like this reaffirmed he had done the right thing in marrying Peyton. Ellie had endured more upheaval than any child her age should have to bear. She deserved a family that could love and support her through life. He only hoped that Peyton's defensiveness on Ellie's behalf this evening showed she felt exactly the same way.

Four

Peyton slipped back into her room, worried that she might be caught eavesdropping on the tender exchange between Galen and Ellie. She hadn't expected it of him, and that shocked her a little.

She reached for a tissue and brushed away her tears. Theirs appeared to be a very special relationship and for some stupid reason it left her feeling as if she was very much an outsider. That had never bothered her before. She'd always been an outsider after the shame of her father's dismissal from Horvath Corporation. Then in the new town they eventually settled in on the Oregon coast, she hadn't fit in, either. She'd had city girl written all over her in the tight-knit community where fishing and tourism were the main industries. Even when she'd gone to Washington for college she'd been an outsider, a fact that had worked in her favor when she'd hidden her pregnancy and subsequent adoption of her baby. Being an outsider came naturally to her now. It afforded her powers of observation she wouldn't have enjoyed otherwise. She even preferred it, she told herself as she reapplied her lipstick before returning to meet Galen for that drink.

But then why did it still have the capacity to hurt so much? Was it that her own child would be around Ellie's age? Was it because each day she was facing all that she'd given away? Peyton slammed a lid on those thoughts before they could drive her crazy. She'd made her choice, the best one she could for her child at the time. Even in the years immediately after the adoption there was no way she could have supported a child. Things had changed now, of course. Her work had paid extremely well at times. And the payday from the exposé on Alice Horvath would be huge, too. Horvath Corporation was global, but the company itself had never been her target. Just Alice. She'd been the one to arbitrarily destroy Peyton's father's career and, consequently, everything about Peyton's life that she'd held dear.

Keep focused, she told herself, sealing away her emotions behind the virtual locked door she always kept them in. She didn't have time to dwell on the child she'd given away; she didn't have time to dwell on the sense of living on the outside edge of everything she'd thought she'd wanted as a child. She had a job to do and she was going to do it. She straightened her shoulders and gave herself a brief nod in the mirror. She had this.

The night air out on the patio was balmy and redolent with the scent of frangipani. Peyton inhaled deeply and sighed out loud.

"Is it always this blissful here?" she asked.

"Yes. Even in the worst weather there's a raw beauty about the place that always gets to me and soothes me deep inside. It's my refuge when life gets too crazy."

"I had no idea you needed one," she commented as she lowered herself into a rattan chair and stared out at the dark purple and midnight blue sea.

"Everyone does from time to time. It's all about having a coping mechanism."

"Then you're luckier than most to have this." She flung her arm out to encapsulate the view beyond them. "I'm sorry about before," she said, deciding to take the bull by the horns. "For implying you were derelict in your duty toward Ellie."

"Apology accepted."

"I was pissy because I missed you, too."

Where the heck had that come from? Peyton swallowed hard, barely able to believe the words she'd just spoken. But she knew they were true. She hated realizing that she'd come to look forward to seeing his sunny smile. The man was addictive and she now totally understood his popularity with her sex. It didn't mean she wanted to jump his bones, but she'd be lying to herself if she didn't admit she found him attractive.

Okay, she was lying to herself that she didn't want

to jump his bones. If their circumstances had been different, a brief fling with Galen Horvath would have been an amusing breath of fresh air. But that wasn't possible and she needed to keep her mind on the game.

"I'm flattered," Galen responded with a slight duck of his head.

Was that a flush of color on his cheeks she discerned in the gentle patio lighting? Surely, she hadn't embarrassed him with her unexpected honesty. Definitely time for a subject change. "So, what do you recommend for a nightcap?"

"Whatever you fancy. I like to unwind with a good cognac from time to time but an Irish whiskey cream on ice works, too."

"I'll go with the Irish whiskey cream on ice."

She watched him as he moved to the small bar off to one side of the covered patio. All his movements were inherently masculine yet graceful at the same time. Her insides clenched on an unexpected wave of need. No matter how sternly she spoke to herself, it seemed her body had a completely different agenda.

Staring at the sea was infinitely safer than staring at her husband, so she turned her gaze back to the water. The clink of ice against the side of a glass heralded his return.

"Tell me more about you," Galen said as he handed her a drink, then pulled a chair up close to hers and sat.

All she had to do was point her toes and she'd be touching him, she realized as she accepted the glass.

It would take a minimum of effort to run her foot up his calf, then higher still. She curled her bare toes tight against the warm tiled floor of the patio before she could act on her imagination.

"What do you want to know?" she hedged before taking a sip of her drink.

"Where did you grow up?"

This could be tricky and potentially lead her into a discussion she wasn't ready to have. "Oh, California for a bit, then Oregon."

"I grew up in California, too, not far from Santa Barbara. You?"

"Oh, nowhere near there," she lied. "Is everyone in your family expected to work for the Horvath Corporation?" she asked, changing the subject.

"Not necessarily, but we all benefit from the company's successes, so it makes sense to contribute to them, too. Some of my cousins work in other fields, though, like Dani. She's a vet in Ojai. But you were supposed to be telling me about yourself."

Peyton had the grace to look abashed. "Sorry, I have a habit of taking charge of conversations. Occupational hazard."

She'd gone too far, too quickly, and hastened to lighten the mood before he closed up on her completely.

"You have a big family. Have you all always been close? I can't imagine what that's like. Part of me envies you. The other part shrinks in horror at the thought of having to share everything with everyone and not having privacy."

Galen laughed. She liked the sound and wanted to make him laugh more. "Well, the only thing, or person, we ever had to share was Nagy, and our grandfather, too, when he was alive. We all lived fairly close to one another, so it was normal for us to cross each other's paths at school or be on the same sports teams. Every Sunday Nagy had an open invitation for everyone to come and visit and eat with her. Still does. It's always slightly chaotic, but it's good to be together when we can attend—to be around the people you know will always have your back, no matter what."

"That must be nice," Peyton said with a touch of envy.

It was one thing to grow up with privilege like Galen had, but another to have that close sense of family, too. Her father had alienated his own family in the early years of his marriage to her mom, who had in turn been disowned for marrying him. Once her mom was gone there had only been the two of them. Her father's bitterness about the circumstances of his life had made him a hard man to live with. Happiness didn't come easily to him even now. Peyton had always hoped that she'd get glimpses of the man he'd used to be before he was let go from Horvath Corporation. The one who'd played with her before dinner and tucked her into bed at night. But after her mother's diagnosis of multiple sclerosis, he'd changed. He'd become intense and driven and distant—and he'd never shaken those traits off since. His bitterness had become such an intrinsic part of him she'd almost forgotten the lighthearted man he'd been so long ago.

"Deep in thought?" Galen prompted her.

"Yeah, not good ones, either. My upbringing was very different from yours. My mom became ill when I was still in elementary school. It changed things at home. Then when we moved to Oregon she got worse."

"I'm sorry."

His simple words, genuinely spoken, struck at her heart. He was a good man. Empathetic without being intrusive.

"It was all a long time ago. I coped."

"So what made you want to be a journalist?"

She laughed. "I used to drive my parents nuts by always wanting to know the why of everything. That need to know and expose everything at its root has never left me."

"That would explain your interrogation style," he teased.

"Hey, I apologized for that."

"No problem. It's good for people to be passionate about what they do."

Passionate. She could so easily be passionate about him. He was a good listener, all too easy on the eye, and he made her want to do things with him she hadn't done in a long time. Her relationships with men were usually short-lived. She didn't give a lot of herself. Physically, sure, no problem, but she wasn't into emotions. And yet, with Galen, she'd already begun to run the gamut of them. She'd expected this to be a very personal assignment and she'd taken strength from the fact that she'd never had trouble keeping her mind on the job before. But there was something about Galen that all too easily distracted her.

She swirled the melting ice in her drink then lifted the glass to her lips to finish it off. "Well, I'm feeling tired. I think it's time to call it a night."

"Yeah, me too. Thanks for helping me unwind. I appreciate it."

"It was a tough day?"

"Yeah, but tomorrow's all about you guys. We'd better get some sleep so we can make the most of it."

"Good idea. What were you thinking for tomorrow?"

"Not sure. Maybe we can let Ellie plan the day."

"She'd like that."

They both stood and Peyton took their empty glasses to the kitchen.

"Leave it," he said, following her. "We do have staff."

"I know, but I'll never get used to people picking up after me. It was drilled into me from an early age to take responsibility for myself. It stuck."

She rinsed the glasses and put them in the dishwasher.

"Good night," she said as she straightened from the dishwasher and started to leave the kitchen.

"Yeah, see you in the morning."

As she passed close by him, she caught the faint scent of his cologne and felt her body react to it. That all-too-familiar tingling in her muscles. The hyperawareness of his proximity. All she had to do was stop in her tracks and turn and face him and she had no doubt he'd do the rest. Instead, she kept walking until she reached her room. Her heart pounded in her chest as she closed the door and leaned against it, trying to understand his effect on her. He was just a man, right?

Peyton pushed away from the door and got ready for bed with the words *Yeah, right* echoing in the back of her mind.

Five

"Come on, sleepyheads!" Galen knocked on first Ellie's and then Peyton's bedroom doors. "We've got a gorgeous day. Let's make the most of it."

"I'm ready!" Ellie said, bounding out of her room and wrapping her arms around his waist in a big hug.

A lump formed in his throat. This kid, she'd been through so much and her strength never failed to amaze him.

"And what exactly are you ready for, kiddo?" he asked, hugging her back.

"Shopping!"

"You want to go shopping today? Anywhere in particular?"

"Ala Moana," Ellie piped up excitedly. "Then lunch on the beach at Waikiki."

"Sounds like a grand plan," Galen answered with a smile.

He made a mental note to book a chopper to fly them over to Oahu after breakfast. As if Ellie could read his mind, she piped up again.

"What's for breakfast?" she asked. "Where's Peyton?"

"Leilani is making pancakes. You want to go help? I'll check on Peyton."

"Pancakes! My favorite!"

And she was gone, just like that. Some days he envied her energy and wondered how on earth he would keep up with her. Galen turned back to Peyton's bedroom door and knocked again. When there was no answer, he carefully opened the door. Her bed was empty, the sheets tangled as if she'd had a restless sleep. Her laptop was open on the desk facing the ocean. Maybe she'd been working during the night, he thought as he went into the room and wandered over to the desk. He started as he heard the bathroom door open behind him.

"Galen? What are you doing in here?"

"Sorry to invade your privacy," he said quickly. "I hope you're decent?"

"Decent enough," Peyton said from close by.

Her arm snaked out and she pushed the laptop closed before he could read what was on the screen. Her bare skin was still sprinkled with droplets of water from her shower, he noted. His mouth dried as the urge to lick those tiny droplets from her flooded his mind.

"Ellie's gone to breakfast. I just wanted to make sure you were up," he continued, turning to face her.

"As you can see, I am."

She was wrapped in nothing but a towel. Granted, the towel was huge, but the knowledge that she was naked beneath it made every cell in his body jump to urgent attention.

"I'll, ah, leave you to get dressed, then. We'll probably be taking off in forty-five minutes."

"Taking off?"

"Ellie has prescribed shopping followed by lunch on the beach at Waikiki."

Peyton shook her head slightly.

"You having second thoughts about today?" he asked.

"No, I just can't quite get used to the idea that you can island-hop on a whim. Don't mind me."

But he did mind her. A gentleman would leave her to dry herself off and get dressed. He did not want to be a gentleman right now.

"Stick with me. You'll get used to anything," he teased with a fake salacious twirl of an imaginary mustache.

She smiled but he noticed it didn't touch her eyes, which had shadows under them. She looked weary. Without thinking, he reached up to cradle her face with one hand.

"You didn't sleep well?"

"Are you saying I look like a hag?"

He chuckled. "That would be the definition of impossible. But you do look tired. Everything okay?"

Her eyes shuttered for a moment. Then she looked directly back at him. "Everything is fine, really. I had a lot going through my head last night, so, no, I didn't sleep well. I decided to do some work instead."

"You're okay for today, though, right?"

"Wouldn't miss it for the world."

He wasn't imagining it. She was saying the right words, but there was no inflection, no meaning or enthusiasm behind them.

"Okay, this time I'm really leaving you to get dressed. I'd better go and make sure Ellie doesn't hoover up all the pancakes."

Peyton nodded and turned back to the bathroom. He watched her go. The woman was a puzzle. And his wife. She was so different from what he'd been expecting in a bride. What had Nagy been thinking when she'd approved their match? On the surface they looked good together; he knew that as surely as he knew his nose sat in the center of his face. But what lay beneath the surface? She wasn't the easiest person to get to know and sometimes he felt as if she didn't want him to know who she was deep down. If that was the case, why had she married? Surely, marriage, especially an arranged marriage, was built on a foundation of common ground. If you couldn't find that common ground because one partner was flat-out withholding everything about themselves, then where did you start?

Galen slid his phone from his pocket as he walked from Peyton's room and called the pilot on standby for the resort to schedule their flight to Oahu. Once that was done, he joined Ellie in the kitchen. He hadn't been there long before Peyton joined them. She must have applied some kind of concealer because the shadows under her eyes weren't so obvious now. She stroked Ellie's hair as she sat down at the table with them.

"Did you leave me any pancakes?" she said, leaning over to bump shoulders with Ellie.

"Of course I did. And bacon, too. Do you like bacon?"

"Everything's better with bacon," Peyton said, nodding fiercely.

Galen felt himself smile. Even though they hadn't known each other long, Ellie and Peyton appeared to have formed a bond already and, he realized, it made him feel less alone on this new journey of parenting a youngster. Quite frankly, this whole parenting thing terrified him. He loved Ellie as if she was his own daughter, had from the moment he'd held her in his arms the week Nick and Sarah had brought her home. He hadn't expected to feel that bond with someone else's child. He hadn't expected to feel that bond with any child, because deep down he'd never expected to have a family of his own.

After seeing Ilya lose his dad and then losing his own father less than a year later to the same congenital heart defect that had also robbed them of their grandfather, Galen had learned firsthand how loving and losing someone could damage a person. Destroy them, too. It had made him fearful of this thing called love and caused him to shield his emotions, to keep things very much on the surface when it came to relationships. He never allowed himself to actually fall in love. But with Ellie it had been different. He'd held that tiny, helpless babe in his arms and known that for her whole life he would be at her service.

He watched Peyton interacting with Ellie as he sipped his coffee and wondered if his love could grow for this woman, too. Attraction certainly had. Even now he felt hyperaware of her and could barely take his eyes from her as she ate her breakfast.

Every movement Peyton made had a purpose; there was nothing about her that was wasteful or flamboyant. Most people he knew talked with their hands to a degree, but Peyton was always physically composed, giving off a sense of calm that he suspected was a front for a much deeper and more complex mind than she had revealed to him yet.

"Earth to Galen!" Ellie's voice intruded on his thoughts. "You know you're staring. Mommy always said that's not polite."

"And she was right, except when a man stares at his wife," Galen said, putting down his coffee mug on the tabletop with a click. He was a little embarrassed to have been caught out by the nine-year-old and met Peyton's gaze across the table. "Isn't that right, Peyton?"

"I guess so. I never gave it much thought."

Galen's phone beeped, distracting him. "Excuse me, ladies, I believe that's our reminder to be at the helipad in about fifteen minutes. Is that long enough for you both to finish getting ready?"

"I'm already ready," Ellie declared. "Although I

haven't got any money. It's going to be hard to shop without money, isn't it?"

"I'll take care of that for you," Galen assured her. "First stop, an ATM. I'll give you an allowance that you can spend on whatever you want."

Peyton's brows drew together and she looked as if she wanted to say something.

"What?" he asked as Ellie got up and left the table to go brush her teeth.

"It's nothing."

"Clearly, it's something. You look as if you disapprove of me giving Ellie an allowance."

"I just wonder how she'll ever learn the value of money if you just give it to her."

"So you think I need to make her work for it? Kind of mean when we're on honeymoon, don't you think?"

"Look, it wasn't my place to say anything but you did ask."

"I did, and don't worry. This is an indulgence, but she won't grow up expecting handouts every five minutes. I never did and I'd like to think my parents set a good enough example to me that I can continue that with Ellie."

"I've offended you. I apologize."

Offended him? Yeah, maybe. She sure knew how to push his buttons, but he wasn't going to make a big deal of it.

"It's okay. You need to know you can talk to me about anything, Peyton. We're a couple. We should be able to discuss stuff. As time goes on, we'll learn to make decisions together. It's new for us both."

She pushed her chair back and picked up her plate, knife and fork. "You're right. I overreacted. I just—"

He waited for her to continue but she shook her head and took her things to the kitchen counter. Galen stood and followed suit.

"You just…?" he prompted.

She shook her head again. "No, it's nothing. I had a very different upbringing, is all."

Peyton pushed by him and he was left watching her retreating back, again. It seemed to be a trend. Just when he thought he was making headway with her and carefully peeling back a layer to expose some truth about her, she slammed that layer back down with superglue. That made him want to try even harder to understand what made his new wife tick— and he was nothing if not persistent.

Peyton watched Ellie skipping just ahead of Galen and her as they meandered along the white sand of Waikiki Beach. The shopping expedition had gone better than she'd expected. Instead of Galen just peeling off bills and giving them to Ellie, he'd made a point of buying her a cute little shoulder bag and a wallet and then given her some cash he'd drawn from an ATM. Then they'd discussed what she wanted to shop for and traipsed around the mall while she compared prices and eventually made a few purchases. He'd been so patient and Peyton found herself admiring his manner with the girl, even going so far as wishing her dad could have been more like him when she was growing up.

But her circumstances had been vastly different and her father had never had the kind of money at his disposal that Galen had.

"I've made a reservation at the restaurant up there." He gestured at a spot up the beach. "I hope you're both hungry."

"Surprisingly, even after that massive breakfast, yes, I am," Peyton answered.

"Galen! Look out there. Can we do that after lunch?" Ellie was pointing to a wharf jutting out from the sand.

"What is it?" Galen asked.

"The boat takes you out to a submarine and you get to go a hundred feet under the water. Can we do it, please?"

"I don't think—" Peyton started.

"Sure," Galen said at the same time.

"You're not serious, are you?" Peyton said.

"Oh, please, Peyton. It'll be such fun," Ellie pleaded, pointing to the giant sandwich board showing pictures of the underwater experience. "Please?"

"You guys can do it without me," Peyton said firmly.

Silence fell between them and Peyton could feel Ellie's disappointment. When the restaurant's maître d' showed them to their beachfront table, Galen snagged Peyton's arm and held her back a little. Ellie looked at them.

"Let me talk to Peyton a minute. You go on to the table. We'll be right there, okay?" Galen suggested to the girl. "It's okay. I've got my eye on you."

Peyton felt her entire body stiffen. What did he

plan to do? Persuade her that she had to do this thing that Ellie so keenly wanted to do. Hell, no.

"Look, you two can go together. I'm quite happy waiting on the beach."

"No, if we do it, we'll all do it. Can you tell me why you're so afraid?"

"I'm not."

"Don't lie to me, Peyton. I saw the way you reacted the moment Ellie suggested it. It's quite safe, you know. They run operations like this in a few locations."

"And I'm sure they can manage to continue without my patronage."

"You don't want to disappoint Ellie, do you?"

Peyton glared at him. "She won't be disappointed if you take her, will she?"

Galen's voice took on a cajoling tone. "Seems to me that yesterday you were all about us spending time together. The three of us, right?"

"You spending all day at work does not compare to me staying on the beach while you and Ellie do the tourist thing."

"Tell me, Peyton. What is it that freaks you out so much? You strike me as an incredibly brave woman. One who wouldn't let the little things get in your way. After all, you agreed to marry me, sight unseen."

"This isn't the same."

She watched as he waved to Ellie, who'd been settled at an umbrella-shaded table and was staring at the two of them.

"We should go and join her," Peyton said, keen to end the discussion.

"Why won't you tell me?" Galen said softly. "Is it really that bad?"

She shivered in the balmy temperature and tried not to think about the incident soon after her mother's diagnosis that had made her so afraid of enclosed spaces.

"Fine, I'll do it."

"You don't need to make it sound like I'm leading you to imminent doom."

"I said I'll do it, okay?"

"I'll be there with you. You won't regret it."

She doubted that very much. At the very least, she hoped she didn't do something to shame herself. Being shut in an old refrigerator by the neighborhood kids growing up had been one thing, but that sense of being closed in, in the dark, and feeling like every last breath of air was being squeezed out of her lungs had been quite another. All she could think about was what her dad had told her the night before. That her mom was slowly dying and one day they'd have to say goodbye to her, so they had to make the most of every minute she had above ground. Thinking about her mom being in a coffin—with no light, no air—had freaked her out and she'd panicked and begun frantically hammering on the door. And then the unthinkable had happened. As she'd begun to believe she was really going to die, she'd peed herself— a fact that didn't go unnoticed when the other kids finally let her out.

The shame of that moment had been bad enough,

but her father's disapproval when she'd run home to tell him what had happened had been what had struck deepest. She could still see the disgust on his face when he realized she'd wet herself. He wasn't interested in why. Wasn't interested in drying her tears. He'd curtly told her to clean herself up and to make sure nothing like that ever happened again. So she had. And she'd avoided enclosed spaces ever since.

"Come on," Galen said, taking her by the hand. "Let's eat."

"I'm not sure that's a good idea before going in the water, is it?" she said half-jokingly, but in actual fact, wondering how the heck she was going to choke anything down at all.

"Hey, sailors do it all the time. It'll be fine, trust me."

"Trust you? I barely know you."

"But we're working on it, right? Building memories together. Getting to know one another. That's what it's all about, isn't it?"

Was it? Maybe for normal people in a normal relationship. But she wasn't there under a normal pretext, and she'd do well to remember that.

Six

He had understood her reluctance to enter the submarine. After all, everyone had their thing that they hated. But he'd underestimated the level of sheer terror that Peyton would experience. The entire journey, her body had been rigid beside him, her hands clenched on her knees—to stop the trembling, no doubt. While Ellie had been wide-eyed with amazement at the world beneath the sea, his gaze had been fixed on Peyton. Eventually, he'd reached across and taken one of her hands in his and begun to gently stroke his fingers across her white knuckles. In tiny increments, he felt the tension in her begin to ease, but even so, she was not relaxed by any standard.

Afterward, on the top deck of the vessel taking them back to shore, he kept their conversation light, alternating between quizzing Ellie about what she'd seen and making sure that Peyton was taking part in the conversation. To give her credit, she was, but he could see her heart wasn't in it and she looked exhausted.

Once they were back at the house, they went down to the beach for their usual afternoon swim, except this time Peyton stayed on the sand watching from behind large sunglasses as he and Ellie cavorted in the gentle waves. When Ellie had had enough, he sent her up to the house to help Leilani bring some drinks and snacks down to them. Once she was merrily on her mission, he flopped down in the sand beside the recliner where Peyton was sitting.

"You okay?" he asked, looking up at her and noting she was no more relaxed now than she had been on the way back from the submarine trip.

"Fine," she answered succinctly.

"Would that be fine-fine, or just fine?" he pressed.

"I'm okay. All right?"

"You did a brave thing today," he said, deciding to take a different tack.

"I wasn't brave. I was terrified."

"And you did it anyway."

"Well, you weren't going to take Ellie unless I went, too. I had to go."

"I'm sorry. I shouldn't have put you through that."

"No, you shouldn't have."

"Peyton?"

"Hmm?"

"Why were you so scared?"

"I told you. I don't like enclosed spaces."

"The jet that got us here was an enclosed space. The chopper we took to Waikiki was an enclosed space. Why the sub?"

She shivered and reached for her sarong, wrapping it around her shoulders as if she was genuinely cold. Kind of hard to believe, given the perpetually warm air that surrounded them.

"I'll go and see if I can help Ellie."

She swung her legs over the side of the lounger, but before she could stand, he caught her hand and held her in place.

"No, stay, please. Leilani will help her. Why won't you open up to me, Peyton? We're husband and wife. We're supposed to learn to understand one another. If you won't let me understand you, how can we make this work?"

He stared at her, watching the emotions that flickered in her troubled blue-gray eyes—noting the taut lines of her body and how she tightened her hands into fists again, the same way she had on the submarine.

"We only met four days ago, Galen. You can't expect to know all my secrets immediately. A woman needs some mystery about her," she said, deflecting the seriousness of his question.

"Mystery is one thing. What you do is probably spy level ten."

She laughed, and he felt his whole body react to the sound. Joy, yes, that he'd brought a smile to her beautiful face, but more than that. A deeper, more intense reaction that made him want to reach out and touch her. To trace the fine line of her collarbone with his fingertips, then his mouth.

"Spy level ten? What are you, twelve years old?"

"Okay, level ten is probably a bit too high. Six, maybe. But seriously, Peyton. I want to get to know you, to understand what makes you tick. To make you happy."

A tinge of color flushed her cheeks. She blinked hard and swallowed before turning her face away from him.

"Look at me, Peyton. Don't keep hiding from me."

She slowly turned back to face him and he reached out to touch her cheek with his forefinger.

"I didn't mean to upset you," he said softly, catching one tear as it spilled from her lashes.

"It's not you—it's me. I'm just tired, that's all. Look, I had a bad experience as a kid. As part of a dare I was shut in an old refrigerator. I panicked. It left me feeling more than a little fragile when it comes to being shut in small spaces."

"How old were you?"

"A little older than Ellie."

"And your parents didn't help you through it?"

"We had just learned my mom had an incurable disease. My dad was all about working hard and trying to keep a roof over our heads."

She hadn't said much but he could read between the lines. They hadn't been there for her. She'd had to deal with the traumatic experience all on her own. It made his heart ache for the little girl she'd been.

"Again, I'm sorry."

"It's not your fault. It's not anyone's fault, to be honest. You just get on with things. Do what you need to do."

"Is that how you deal with everything in life? Do what you need to do?"

"Mostly."

"Is that why you married me?"

"No!" she protested. "That's different."

"Tell me, Peyton. What do you expect from our marriage?"

"What everyone expects," she hedged without going into any details. "Oh, look, there's Ellie and Leilani."

He wasn't mistaken—there was a distinct note of relief in her voice as they watched the two approach from the path leading to the house. Okay, he'd let her have her retreat, but he wasn't going to stop delving beneath the surface of what made her tick. Because at some point today, he'd realized that he really wanted to understand his new wife properly. Understand her and, hopefully, make this a proper marriage.

The next morning Peyton gave herself a stern pep talk in the mirror. No more weakness, no more frailty. Certainly no more exposing any softness to Galen. He'd been so persistent down on the beach yesterday. She couldn't afford to allow any further cracks to show. She was here for vengeance, nothing else.

She settled her features into what she hoped was a serene expression and squared her shoulders, ready to face the day. Ellie was just outside her door as she left her room.

"Good morning. Did you sleep well after yesterday? No bad dreams about sharks and shipwrecks?"

Ellie laughed. "No, I loved it. I don't remember dreams most times I wake up. Sometimes I dream about Mom and Dad, though. That they're still alive. When I wake up from those dreams I always feel sad. Sometimes I wish I could stay asleep just to be with them again."

Peyton reached out and stroked Ellie's hair. "I can understand that. I still dream about my mom, too, and she died a long time ago. You can always talk to me about it, if you want to."

What the heck was she doing? She didn't want to establish too strong a rapport with Ellie because she wasn't planning on sticking around. The poor girl had already had her world ripped out from under her—she didn't need to begin relying on someone who didn't plan on being around for longer than the requisite three-month trial period of the marriage.

"Or Galen, you can always talk to him," she added hastily.

"Who's talking about me?" Galen asked as he came down the hallway. "Ah, my two best girls. That's okay, then."

Ellie giggled and skipped toward him to give him a hug. "What are we doing today?"

"Well, as luck would have it, I think I've found the perfect escape for you."

"Escape?" Ellie looked confused. "I'm not a prisoner. Why do I need to escape?"

"I know you're not," Galen said. "You can totally leave at any time."

"No, I can't!" Ellie laughed.

"True, but today you can, if you want to, have some company from someone your age."

"You won't leave me there, will you?"

"Of course not. I don't plan on leaving you anywhere you don't want to be. The resort manager here has a daughter your age and she's really looking forward to meeting you. She has a pony."

Peyton watched as the caution on Ellie's face was replaced with rapt attention.

"A pony? When can we go?"

"After breakfast. We'll take you there, and if you're happy with it, we'll leave you to your girlie stuff and come back and pick you up after lunch. Deal?"

"Deal!"

Ellie flew down the hall toward the kitchen, where she would no doubt scoff her breakfast and be ready in record time.

"Well played," Peyton said.

"What do you mean?"

"Mentioning a pony. I don't think there are many girls Ellie's age who aren't enamored of ponies."

He shrugged. "I didn't want her getting bored, is all. She could do with a bit of fun with someone her own age."

"What about you? What do you plan to do?" Peyton asked.

"I thought I'd take my wife sailing."

She loved to sail. The freedom of being on the water, as opposed to yesterday's expedition under it, held huge appeal for her. Skimming the waves, the wind in her hair, the crack of the sails as they caught the wind—she loved every aspect of it. It was a freedom she'd been introduced to as an adult but didn't get to experience often.

"Okay. I'll come, but only if you let me take the helm."

"Control freak," he goaded gently.

"Maybe," she replied with a grin.

"You drive a hard bargain but never let it be said I'm a man who won't let a woman take charge."

Was that a hint of innuendo in his voice? Peyton looked sharply at him, trying to ascertain whether or not to take his words at face value. "Are you patronizing me?" she asked slowly.

"I would never be so rude. No, I merely meant what I said. You forget, it was my grandmother who ran Horvath Corporation after my grandfather passed away. I'm not afraid of strong women. I revere them."

He was right about his grandmother being a strong woman. Knowing how much he respected the old lady, maybe she could get him to open up a bit more about her while they were sailing?

"Good to know," she said with a semi-smile.

Ellie had finished her breakfast by the time they joined her.

"Whoa! Hold on a minute. Are you sure you've

actually eaten?" Galen teased her before she raced off to brush her teeth.

"I did! Should I get changed in case we do ride? I don't have any gear with me." All of a sudden Ellie looked unsure of herself.

"You look gorgeous as you are but maybe take a day pack with your swimsuit as well as jeans suitable for riding. I know there are spare helmets and boots at the stables, so you'll be fine."

Confidence restored, Ellie took off back to her room.

"You're really very good with her," Peyton observed.

"We're a work in progress. I'm constantly worried that I'm going to mess up but at least now I have company in this parenting thing."

Peyton felt a sudden pressure on her chest. "If our marriage works out."

"Why wouldn't we work out?"

"Well, you know. We might find we can't stand the sight of each other after three months. Earlier, even."

She knew she sounded like she was grasping at straws, but it had to be said.

"Cold feet already, Peyton?"

His face had grown serious and his blue eyes bored into hers as if he could see past the facade and deep into the secrets she was keeping.

"Not exactly. Just being practical."

Galen took a step closer to her. "For the record, I really enjoy the sight of you every morning and every evening, too, not to mention the hours in between."

His voice caressed her like a physical touch and Peyton set her nerve endings on edge. How did he do that? The sound of his voice had a power over her she'd never experienced with anyone before. She caught the subtle scent of his cologne and, despite herself, inhaled deeply.

"In fact," he continued, "I like a lot about you, and I really want to know you better. You just need to let go a little."

"Let go?"

"Yeah, you hold everything about yourself so tightly inside. You don't let people in, not even Ellie."

"I don't want her hurt if this doesn't work out."

"Why focus on the negative? Why not think about the benefits to all of us if it does work out?"

There was something about the way he said *benefits* that sent a surge of need through her body. She swallowed against the involuntary sound that rose in her throat and silently prayed that her hardened nipples were not painfully obvious through her light T-shirt.

"I'm ready!"

Ellie's voice behind her made her start and come back to her senses. Of course Galen hadn't meant anything like the benefits her runaway hormones wanted. Or had he? There was a mischievous gleam in his eye now that wasn't there before. Oh yes, he was well aware of the train of her thoughts, and their effect on her body.

"Excellent work, kiddo. I'll drive you over to their house in a moment. Just let me get my keys."

He was back in under a minute. "Okay, let's go."

"You haven't had your breakfast yet," Peyton pointed out as she settled at the table and helped herself to toast and scrambled eggs that Leilani had left on a covered warmer for them.

"I'll be back in ten. I'll eat then."

"Galen?" Ellie said.

"Hmm?"

"Why don't you and Peyton kiss when you say bye, like Mommy and Daddy always did?"

A sensation, not unlike icy-cold water, ran down Peyton's spine.

"Maybe Peyton can answer that," Galen offered, looking at her with the light of challenge in his eyes.

"We don't know each other as well as your mommy and daddy did," Peyton said awkwardly.

"My mommy said that Daddy kissed her on their very first date and she knew then that she was going to marry him. You two should kiss, too, and hold hands. That's what married people do, right?"

"I, ah…" Peyton's voice trailed off as she tried to think of something suitable to say.

"Like this?" Galen asked.

Peyton stiffened as Galen bent down and brushed her cheek with his lips. She felt a sense of intense relief when he left it at that.

"No, silly, like they do in the movies," Ellie said with a giggle.

"Oh, like this, you mean?"

Peyton wasn't ready for it. In fact, in a million years she'd never be ready for it, but he did it anyway. Galen bent down again and, tipping her chin up with one hand, took her lips in a kiss that honestly made her toes curl and her gut clench on another of those irritating surges of desire. He teased her lips open, deepening their kiss as her senses went into overdrive. Their only points of contact were his fingers at her chin and his lips on hers and yet her entire body went up in flames. For a moment she lost all sense of where she was, not to mention who was watching, and when Galen pulled back she was left feeling breathless with her mind spinning out of control.

That shouldn't have happened. The kiss. Her reaction. Any of it.

"Exactly like that," Ellie chortled from the other side of the room.

"Good to know," Galen replied with a quick grin before directing his next words to Peyton. "I'll be back soon. Try not to miss me too much."

And then, with a wink, he was gone.

Seven

Galen listened to Ellie chattering excitedly to him all the way to the resort manager's house and knew he was making the right responses, but internally he was in turmoil. Kissing Peyton like that had started as a bit of fun, and maybe to put a lid on Ellie's questions. But what the hell had he been thinking? What was supposed to be a sweet kiss had rapidly turned into a full-on assault on his equilibrium.

Yes, he'd begun to think he wanted more than a simple companionable marriage with Peyton, but this was something else entirely. That kiss had ignited a hunger in him that, now woken, would only continue to demand. And what if those demands weren't met? He wasn't about to force Peyton into anything that she didn't want. The very idea turned his stomach. But she'd been a willing participant in that kiss they'd just had, and that gave him hope—a great deal of hope—that with careful handling, theirs could become a real marriage. One with a strong physical connection.

He'd observed Valentin with his wife, and Ilya with his. When they were in the same room with their respective spouses it was as if there was an invisible current that ran between them. A link that couldn't be broken. He'd never thought for a minute that he wanted that kind of link with someone else. Oh, sure. He'd enjoyed relationships in the past, but he'd never wanted the depth of connectedness that his brother and cousin shared with their wives—until now. And now that he wanted it, he needed to figure out how to get it because, on the surface, Peyton had entered their marriage on similar terms to his. She hadn't mentioned wanting a grand passion; getting her to say what she wanted was a mission in itself.

It was a good thing he was man enough for the mission, he told himself as he pulled up outside the resort manager's house. He and Ellie got out of the car and were greeted by the resort manager and his daughter. When Galen was certain Ellie was comfortable with them and had arranged the time to pick her up, he headed back to the house feeling oddly nervous.

As far as he could see, no one remained happy in a marriage without some form of physical closeness—whether it was a grand passion or something more companionable. Based on how Peyton had reacted to their kiss, he knew she was capable of the former, although it left him wondering why she'd want to settle for anything less.

Peyton was in the kitchen when he got back. She'd obviously been busy. A packed hamper and cooler sat on the table.

"I wasn't sure what you wanted for our boat ride, so I just made sandwiches and grabbed some fruit and snacks and drinks."

Normally, Peyton appeared serene, untouchable. Right now she looked uncertain, as if she needed his reassurance. He hastened to give it to her.

"Sounds perfect. I was going to ask Leilani to do that for us, but since you've already done it, we can head straight to the marina. Have you packed your swimsuit?"

"I'm wearing it under this," she said, gesturing to her clothing.

He spied the ties of a halter snaking up from the neckline of her T-shirt. Did that mean she was wearing a two-piece today? His blood pressure kicked up a notch. Until now she'd been wearing a one-piece, and he had the distinct feeling that seeing her in a bikini could well undo him.

He grabbed the hamper and cooler and led the way back out to the car.

"You don't need us to grab towels or anything?" Peyton said, hanging back a little.

"Everything we need is on the boat," he answered.

"Just how big is this boat?" Peyton asked.

"She's thirty-six feet. Good for blue-water sailing but I rarely have time for that these days."

"Wow, that's a lot bigger than I was thinking."

"You'll love it. If you've enjoyed sailing on a smaller yacht, you'll really have fun on this one."

She fell silent and he could almost hear the cogs turning in her head.

"What is it?" he prodded her.

"Nothing, except... I guess I just can't quite get used to everything you seem to take for granted."

He frowned slightly. "Hey, don't get me wrong. I might be accustomed to a high standard of living, but trust me, I don't take one moment of it for granted. I saved darn hard for *Galatea* and bought her when I was in my early twenties. She was my first ever major acquisition and I felt so incredibly proud of myself the first time I took her out."

"Galatea is the goddess of calm seas in Greek mythology, isn't she?"

"Yeah, that's right. You're a fan of Greek mythology?"

"I did some papers on it in relation to classical literature in college."

"Sounds heavy," he said as he approached the car and opened the passenger door for her.

"It was. I think I preferred the fairy-tale versions of mythology told to me when I was a kid."

There was a wistful tone to her voice that prompted him to remain silent. Was she starting to open up a little more? He watched as she wrinkled her nose and grimaced briefly.

"But life's not about fairy tales, is it? Mythology is based on many brutal and sad stories."

"Some would say modern journalism isn't far different."

"Except it's based in exposing truth, not make-believe."

"Is that what appeals to you about your work? Getting to the core of things?"

He'd done some Google searches at night when he couldn't sleep for wondering about the woman sleeping down the hallway from him. Several of her articles were online and he'd been struck by the raw honesty in them. She didn't hold back from telling the truth, which was why she presented such a conundrum to him in real life. If writing in nitty-gritty detail was such an intrinsic part of her, why was she so selective about what she chose to reveal to him in person?

"You could say that. I hate injustice on any level. It needs to be exposed and the people perpetrating it held accountable for their actions."

Galen put the car into gear and headed down the driveway, surprised at the simmering anger in her tone.

"I read your piece on migrant workers. It was good," he said, opting for conversational safe ground.

"Thank you. I was rather proud of that assignment."

"So you're completely freelance?"

"Yes, I prefer being able to pick and choose my projects. It's a freedom that I worked hard to attain. Now I feel like I'm really doing what I was called to do."

"I'm glad for you. Everyone should be able to do what they love, right?"

* * *

Peyton felt the familiar anger toward Alice Horvath bubble in her veins. Yes, everyone should be able to do what they loved and not be persecuted and have false accusations made against them. She closed her eyes and took a steadying breath. She couldn't let her emotions get the better of her or she might slip up. This particular assignment was all too close to her heart and she wanted to give it her best. Her best meant never letting her guard down around the man sitting next to her, steering the sleek convertible toward the marina.

"It's a privilege to be able to do so. Not one I take for granted. I guess I'm a bit like you in that regard."

"Good to know we have some things in common," he answered lightly.

He pulled up in a parking lot beside rows and rows of berthed vessels. The sheer wealth exhibited here should have disgusted her but she couldn't help thinking of how much joy each of these symbols of exclusivity brought to the people who owned them, not to mention the jobs created building and outfitting them.

"We both breathe air, that's another thing," she said, her voice dry.

As she expected, Galen burst out laughing. "I would hope we have more in common than that," he said, still chuckling as he retrieved the hamper and cooler from the trunk and led her down one of the jetties toward a gleaming white-and-blue yacht.

"She's beautiful," Peyton said, pointing out the elegantly scripted name on the back of his yacht.

"My first true love."

"And your second?"

He stepped across onto the deck and held a hand out to assist her. His eyes met hers. "I'll let you know."

Peyton's throat dried and she swallowed hard. Was he implying he was falling in love with *her*? Surely not. It was too soon. Besides, he'd said at the wedding he wasn't looking for that kind of relationship.

But then there was that kiss. Peyton assured herself he had only done that to satisfy Ellie. It wasn't as if he had wanted to do it; he'd been coerced. And she certainly hadn't wanted it, either. She'd been taken completely by surprise. She couldn't lie to herself, though. It had been one heck of a kiss. Even now, just thinking about it made her press her lips together as if she could re-create the sensations he'd drawn from her.

She followed Galen through a hatch that led to a well-appointed galley and seating area below deck. He stripped off his shirt and dropped it on a squab in the dining area. In the close quarters, with him now wearing nothing but a pair of boat shoes and swim shorts, and without Ellie here as chaperone, Peyton was almost afraid of what she might do. Repeat the kiss of this morning, perhaps? More, even? Like, reach out and touch him—discover if he was as hot to touch as she felt right now?

"How about I put everything away for you," she blurted. "You get us going."

"Sure, but before we do, could you put sunblock on my back? I did everywhere else this morning."

Couldn't he just keep his shirt on? She mentally

rolled her eyes. She didn't even know why she was reacting like this. She'd done it for him already a few times when they'd been down on the beach. But that was before they'd kissed.

"I promise I'll return the favor," he said, handing her the tube of lotion.

"I, ah… I thought I might keep my shirt on today," she said, taking the lotion from him and squirting a liberal amount into her palm.

"Sure, that works. As long as you don't mind that scratchy feeling of wearing it home after we've been snorkeling."

He had a point. Why did he have to go and kiss her like that this morning? It had changed everything. She began to rub the lotion onto his back, smoothing it along his lean, powerful shoulders and massaging it down the long muscles that lined his spine. He stood there like a statue, seemingly immune to her touch, while all the time her palms and fingertips tingled and her hands ached to travel around his waist to his belly and up to his chest—and then lower. So maybe the kiss had only changed everything for her.

She slapped him on the shoulder. "You're done."

Galen turned slowly. Okay, so maybe she wasn't the only one feeling the heat.

"Take off your shirt," he commanded.

Her eyes flicked back up to his face. Yes, that had been a command. The man looked determined. She spun slowly around and slipped off her T-shirt. The contrast of cold lotion and his very warm hands made her gasp as he began to apply the sunblock to her skin.

His long, smooth, sure strokes made every muscle in her body tense in anticipation.

"Lift your arms," he instructed, his voice not sounding as confident as usual.

She did as he said and her breath caught in her throat as he smoothed sunblock on her sides, almost, but not quite, touching her breasts as he did so. Her nipples had bunched into aching peaks and every nerve was attuned to his touch. And then he stopped. She didn't know whether to rejoice or be disappointed.

"I'll go start up the motor and get ready to cast off."

Again, his voice held that strange note. At least he could speak. Words totally failed her. If he'd turned her around and kissed her again she doubted they'd have made it out of the marina today.

She looked toward the stateroom beyond where she stood. To the very large bed that stretched from one wall of the room to the other. She snatched her gaze away and schooled her thoughts.

She heard the sound of his feet on the steps leading to the deck and finally allowed her body to relax. It was no good, though. She could still feel the aftereffects of his touch on her skin. The sureness of his long fingers. His heat, which had ignited a simmering cauldron inside her. She stared unseeing at the picnic hamper to be unpacked. She needed to move but it was as if she was locked in a sensual trap, held captive by her own wants.

Eight

Galen kept his hands fisted around the wheel as he guided *Galatea* from her berth and out of the marina. Walking away from Peyton just now was one of the hardest things he'd ever had to do. Every instinct in his body and his mind had urged him to turn her around and pull her to him. To feel the heat of her skin against his. To lower his lips to her mouth and kiss her again. To find out whether those crazy fireworks that had ignited this morning were nothing more than an aberration.

But he knew if he'd done that, he wouldn't have known where to stop. They'd likely have ended up in the bed on board the yacht, and he wanted to know that when they came together she came willingly and with as much hunger for him as he had for her.

That day would come, he consoled himself as he fought to get his body and his thoughts back under control. He needed to keep his focus on the job at hand, which was negotiating past the breakwater out into the sea. Galatea had woven her magic, he noted, as the sea was serenely calm today. A complete contrast to the way his mind felt right now.

He saw Peyton come up on deck. "Can I get you anything?" she asked, looking hesitant.

"Perhaps you'd like to take the wheel while I get the sails ready."

"Sure."

Even with the gentle sea breeze brushing past his body like a lover's caress, he could feel the warmth that came off her as she came to stand beside him.

"I have a confession to make," she said ruefully as she stared at the wheel.

"And that is?"

"I've never steered a boat as big as this before."

"You'll be fine. The principle is the same."

He quickly gave her a few instructions, concluding with, "So when I give you a shout, you can turn off the motor."

She was a quick study, he noted, when a short time later the sound of the engine died away and the only noise around them was the wind catching in the sails.

"This is incredible," Peyton said with a laugh.

He looked at her beautiful face and smiled in return. For the first time since he'd met her, she looked completely relaxed. He wanted to see her like this more often. Open and carefree, instead of closed and, dare he say it, suspicious. He realized the latter attitude may come with the territory in her line of work. But right now she was happy, and he'd bask in that for as long as it lasted.

After sailing for an hour or so, they took down the sails and put down anchor near a small, sheltered bay. They ate their lunch and lay on the deck for a while, soaking up the sun.

"This is blissful. Ellie would have enjoyed it," Peyton commented, shading her eyes from the sun as she rolled over onto her back.

"The last time she came out on *Galatea* was with her mom and dad. She has happy memories on the water. I might see about bringing the yacht back to Port Ludlow for the summer."

"You can do that? It's a long way to sail. Doesn't it scare you?"

"If I plan it right, nothing will go wrong. I bring a small crew with me on repositioning trips. You could come, too."

"I think I'll take a pass on that."

"Chicken?"

"No." She shifted to a sitting position and wouldn't quite meet his eyes. "I can't make plans that far in advance. I don't know what I'll be doing by then."

It was as if the sun had disappeared behind a cloud. He sat up, too. "What do you mean?"

"Well, I could be away on an assignment," she said, sounding slightly flustered.

"You're still planning to work away from home?"

"I still have a job to do, Galen. You'll still be doing

yours, won't you? That requires business trips from time to time, doesn't it?"

She had a point but deep down inside he knew he'd be putting Ellie and Peyton's needs before any business trips going forward. At least that was his plan. Peyton, it seemed, didn't intend to change her life even though they were now married. So what had she been looking for in this marriage?

"We're going to have to coordinate our schedules carefully now that we're married," he conceded. "We can't leave Ellie holding down the fort alone. But we'll figure it out. I wanted to talk to you about having a live-in housekeeper anyway, once we find a new home."

"I guess I'd have to be okay with that, wouldn't I?"

"You mean you could get used to someone picking up after you, after all?" he teased.

"Or we could all get used to pulling our weight around the house to help her out, right?"

The tension that had built between them began to fade and a companionable silence took its place. After a while Galen got up and headed below deck. When he came back on top, he had snorkeling gear in his hands.

"This is a beautiful bay for snorkeling. Have you tried it before?" he asked, passing her a mask, snorkel and pair of fins. "I think these should suit you. Let's try them for fit."

"Can't say I've had the pleasure."

"There's nothing to it. All you need to remember when you go under water is that when you resurface you have to blow out hard to clear the pipe before you breathe in again. And if you don't want to go under water, you can float along the surface and still see a lot."

"That sounds more like my style," she said, trying the mask on for size. "How do I look?"

"Like a mutant goldfish, but that seal around your face looks good."

He quickly showed her how to clear the mask if water seeped in and helped her put on her fins before doing the same himself. Then he showed her how to step off the transom at the back of the yacht and into the sea.

Half an hour later they were back on board and Peyton was voluble in her delight.

"Did you see that turtle? That was incredible!"

He smiled indulgently. Yes, bit by bit he was starting to see the real Peyton Earnshaw. And the more natural and unforced she became, the more he wanted to know about her.

They were back at the marina tidying up the yacht when Galen's cell phone began to chime. It brought home to Peyton exactly how long they'd been out alone together today. The earlier sexual tension had eased off—not completely, but certainly enough for her to be able to relax and enjoy the experience. There were definitely some benefits to being married to a man who appeared to have everything, she conceded to herself with a grin.

"Peyton? It's Ellie on the phone."

Suddenly, her sense of well-being was put on hold. "Is everything all right?"

"Yeah, she's fine. She wanted to know if she can sleep over with Caitlin. Seems they're getting on like a house on fire. Caitlin's mom and dad are cool with it."

"Well, it's your call, isn't it?"

"We're in this together," he reminded her.

"It's okay by me," Peyton said stiffly, uncomfortable to be included in what was obviously a very parental decision.

Galen turned his attention back to the call, which lasted another two minutes. "Well, that's one very happy little girl," he said as he came below to collect the hamper and cooler.

"I take it she isn't usually a fan of sleepovers?"

"Not recently, no. This break away from home has been good for her. It's a relief to see her feel relaxed and trust that everything will be okay with us while she's with Caitlin and her parents."

"I hated sleepovers as a kid."

Oh heavens, why had she blurted that out? Now he'd want to know why. Of course, that was the very next question out of his mouth. Peyton gathered her thoughts together before answering, deciding brief and honest was probably the best approach.

"I guess, at the heart of it, I was always scared I'd get home and find out my mom had died and I wasn't there."

The words hurt to say and she wished she'd never opened this can of worms.

"That must have been hard."

"You get used to it. Your dad died, too. That can't have been easy."

"No, it wasn't, but I was in my teens, and while his death came as a shock, we didn't have the fear of it constantly hanging over us. We probably should have, though. My grandfather and my uncle both died of the same congenital heart defect before him."

"Did he never get checked out?"

"He always said he was too busy. Of course, Nagy made sure everyone in the family had a full medical workup after my father's death. Only one of my cousins has inherited the same problem but it's well managed now they're aware of it."

"Must have been worrying, wondering if you all carried the same time bomb."

"It was, but Nagy took care of it—of all of us. As she does."

Peyton felt the customary bristle of anger when she heard him speak of his grandmother in glowing terms. But this was a natural opportunity to find out more about the woman who'd had such a devastating effect on her family.

"She's very much the matriarch, isn't she? Does everyone obey her?"

Galen laughed. "You say that as if she sits on a throne and dictates orders to us all."

"Well, doesn't she? From what you say, she's omnipotent."

His face took on a softer look. "No, she's human,

just like the rest of us. And she makes mistakes, with her own health, no less."

"So it's a matter of do as I say, not as I do?"

"Kind of like that. You probably heard she had a serious heart attack a few months ago. We're all so grateful that Valentin was there when it happened. He did CPR until an ambulance could get there. She's been different since. As if she thinks she's living on borrowed time but she still has so much to complete before her time is up. There's a weird urgency about her. It's kind of hard to explain."

"I guess a near-death experience will change a person."

"That's for sure."

They went up on deck. Galen locked the cabin door behind them before they left the yacht and headed back to the car. Peyton rued the fact she'd lost her opportunity to keep the conversation on Galen's relationship with his grandmother but filed away the snippets he'd already disclosed.

Once they got back to the beach house, she showered and changed, then typed up her notes from the conversation. When she was finished, she walked out onto the patio.

Through the open doors she could hear Galen on a call, so she settled on a sun lounger in the shade and let the beauty of the day and her surroundings lull her into sleep. She was surprised to see how low the sun was when she woke to the sound of the tinkle of ice cubes in a pitcher being put on the table in front of her.

"That had better be margaritas," she said sleepily.

"How did you know?" Galen asked, putting two chilled, salt-rimmed glasses down on the table beside the pitcher.

"Because that's just what I feel like. After a big glass of water, anyway."

"Then it's just as well that's what I made. Predinner cocktails. Did you have a good sleep?"

"I can't believe I slept that long. Why didn't you wake me?"

He shrugged with a casual elegance. "You looked like you needed it. A day on the water can be tiring."

"I bet you didn't sleep."

Again, that shrug. He poured the drinks, handed her a glass and held his toward her in a toast. "Here's to more days like today."

She clinked her glass to his. "Indeed."

Then she remembered the kiss. Did he mean *all* of today? She met his gaze as she took a sip of the perfectly blended cocktail. Oh yes, he totally did.

Suddenly, this whole marriage thing felt too complicated. She honestly hadn't thought this through. She'd imagined that she'd cruise through the first three months without worrying about fighting off a growing physical attraction or having to ignore the magnetism that steadily grew stronger between them, and she'd write her article then extract herself as neatly as she'd gotten into it.

He was a Horvath. A direct descendant of the person who'd upended everything that was safe and secure in Peyton's world and set her up for hardship.

Yes, she'd clawed her way beyond that hardship now, but it had been a hard road and full of sacrifice.

For the briefest moment she allowed herself to think of the beautiful baby girl she'd had to give up and felt the all-too-familiar pain those thoughts always brought. That was what she needed to keep front and center in her mind. Pain. Loss. Disappointment. It was the only defense she had against the almost overwhelming enticement that was Galen Horvath.

Nine

It was a good thing they would be heading home in two days, Peyton thought as they finished their dinner on the patio. It was far too easy to be seduced by the stunning beauty of both this place and the man sitting opposite her.

The meal he'd prepared for the two of them while she'd been sleeping was perfection. The shrimp kebab appetizer had been mouthwatering, and the baked fish he'd served with a Greek salad as their main course had been outstanding.

"Do you feel like dessert? Leilani left a mango cheesecake in the refrigerator."

"Oh, no. I couldn't fit in another bite," Peyton protested. "In fact, I may never need to eat again. That was truly amazing. I had no idea you could cook."

"One of my hidden talents. To be honest, as a bachelor, I learned to cook food I enjoyed a long time ago. Now cooking is more of a way to relax for me than a necessity."

She narrowed her eyes a little. "And you needed more relaxation after today?"

He laughed and she felt her lower belly tighten. It didn't matter how many times she heard the sound; his laughter always had this effect on her.

"You can never have too much relaxation. How about a nice slow stroll on the beach?" he asked, holding out his hand to her as he stood up from the table.

She accepted his hand and let him help her up, expecting him to let go as they started on the path down to the beach. But he kept her hand clasped lightly in his and, despite her earlier reminders to herself to keep her distance, she liked it. The waves murmured softly against the sand as they strolled along the beach. The night was so perfect. It was a shame everything about being here was fake, she told herself, trying desperately not to fall under its spell.

But it was impossible not to, especially when Galen stopped and dropped to the sand, tugging her down with him so she was cradled between his legs and leaning against his strong chest and tight stomach. She tried not to relax, to keep herself ever so slightly apart from him, but she failed miserably. The lure of his warm body against her back—the feeling of being sheltered, protected—it was all too much. Galen traced his fingers along her arm, sending a rash of goose bumps along her skin.

"Cold?" he asked.

"No."

She was anything but cold. In fact, his every touch heated her blood more and more. To distract herself she tried to dig more information out of him about his family.

"Tell me about growing up," she asked. "Were you a little beach boy?"

"I've always been drawn to the water, that's true. Growing up was, well, fun. As a kid we didn't know what trouble was unless we broke a window or talked back to an adult."

"Sounds idyllic."

"Isn't that what childhood is supposed to be? Free of adult worries? How about you? You've mentioned a few dark spots, but surely it wasn't all bad?"

Had it all been bad? Not if she was honest. Before her mom got ill, and her father was disgraced, their life had been so very different. She searched her past, latching on to one particular memory that had brought her incredible joy.

"My happiest memory of my childhood was the day my dad brought home a puppy," she said softly.

"That sounds like it would have been a very happy memory. What was the puppy like?"

"He was a mutt, medium sized and very boisterous. I loved him so much."

"And?" Galen coaxed her a little more.

"And when my mom got sick and my dad lost his job, we had to move and surrender him to a local shelter. We couldn't afford to keep him anymore."

And just like that, the rift in her heart opened up again. She'd suppressed memories of Bingo and the part he'd played in her life. When her mom had gotten sick, Bingo had been her confidant. Listening faithfully as she poured out her worries, letting her cry into his springy fur when it all got too much.

"That was rough," Galen sympathized, pressing a kiss on her head.

"I got over it. At least I knew at the no-kill shelter my mom insisted on, he'd be rehomed, and he was such a lovely dog. He didn't stay there long."

But it was yet another loss she could lay at Alice Horvath's door, Peyton reminded herself. Yet another reason to expose exactly how far Alice's cruelties extended.

The breeze picked up, blowing strands of hair onto Peyton's face. Galen brushed them behind her ear. His touch was a sizzle of electricity across her skin. Peyton didn't want to talk anymore. Right now she wanted to forget the memories that had reopened old wounds and lose herself in the man who was here with her. She shifted slightly so she faced Galen. His eyes locked with hers as she lifted her hand to cup his cheek. And then she leaned forward to kiss him.

The shock of touching his lips with hers, of taking charge and of giving in, shot through her like a bolt from above. Soon, both her hands were locked behind his head as she kissed and nibbled at his lips. He kissed her back. Hot, wet and everything she needed to obliterate her painful past and live in the moment.

Somehow, they ended up lying on the sand, his

body half over hers. She pressed her hips up, grinding against him and earning a groan from deep in his throat in response. He was rock-hard, his body straining toward hers, but even though he so clearly wanted her, he didn't press home the advantage. Instead, he held himself away from her slightly. Leaning on one elbow, he stroked her with his free hand, slowly moving the fabric of her skirt up over her thighs.

She shivered at his touch, wanting more. Wanting him. She'd been fighting this attraction from the moment she first saw him, but right now she was incapable of pushing him away.

His fingers softly caressed her inner thighs and she moaned, her hips involuntarily pushing upward again. Her hands still clasped his head, and his mouth was still on hers, their kisses long and drugging, sending a sensual spiral through her brain. She felt his fingers trace the edge of her panties and the hollowed curve at her groin. It was one of her most sensitive places and she moaned again, her body tensing for that moment when he'd move aside the fabric and touch that part of her that ached for his possession.

Galen shifted slightly, taking his lips from hers and kissing a line along her jaw, then down her throat and across her collarbone. Her body went liquid as he continued his sensual assault; her skin was ultra-sensitive, her mind focused on the pleasure he drew from her. She lifted her hips again, silently urging him to touch her where she most needed, her hands moving to stroke the back of his neck, his shoulders, down his back.

Beneath her fingertips she felt the corded muscles of his body, their tension a mark of his restraint as he touched and kissed her—his focus purely on her pleasure alone. And then his hand moved to her mound, cupping her through the lace, his finger pressing unerringly on her clitoris and sending a piercing pleasure through her. She felt herself grow wet with need.

A particularly large wave suddenly crashed onto the beach, the sound roaring through her consciousness and reminding her of where they were. Of what they were doing. She stiffened, pulling away immediately.

"What is it?" Galen asked, his voice husky with desire.

"We can't do this," Peyton said abruptly and shoved him away for good measure.

"Okay," he answered carefully. "Shall we go back to the house?"

"I don't know about you but I'm going back."

Peyton scrambled to her feet and began to stride as fast as she could down the beach, dusting the sand off her as she went. How could she have been so stupid as to give in to her personal needs? This whole exercise was not about her. She couldn't afford to indulge in her desires. She was here to collect information.

But even as she worked her way through the soft whispering sand and to the path that led to their holiday house, her subconscious was urging her to stop and look back. To see if Galen followed her. To turn back to him and continue what they'd started. She shut down the treacherous thoughts before they could take a firm hold and bloom into something she knew she'd regret.

When she got to her room, she slammed her door hard and locked it for good measure. She didn't for one minute believe that Galen would try to enter her room or ever dream of forcing himself on her, or anyone, for that matter. She might symbolically be shutting him out, but if she was being truly honest, she was shutting herself in because right now she could barely trust herself around him anymore.

Today had been a mistake from start to finish. First the kiss, then the sailing, then the idiotically romantic walk on the beach after an equally romantic meal together. Even just thinking about it made her want to turn around and head back out that door and find him again. Pretty much every cell in her body was calling her every kind of stupid for leaving herself hanging like that when Galen had been so close to giving her the pleasure her body craved.

Peyton stomped across her room and into the bathroom, snapping on the shower faucet and shucking off her clothes, leaving them at her feet. She had to scrub this urge out of her right now, before she did something idiotic like follow her instincts. She wasn't here to fall in lust with the man and she certainly wasn't going to allow herself to do anything as dumb as fall in love.

All love ever did was hurt people and she wasn't going down that road ever again.

The flight back to SeaTac was smooth but Galen still couldn't shake the questions that filled his mind over Peyton's desertion the other night. Things had been coming along nicely between them. He knew she'd been there with him every step of the way. After all, hadn't she been the one to start it in the first place? And then nothing. It was as if she'd turned herself off like a tap. The next time he'd seen her, over breakfast the next morning, she'd been even more distant than before and she'd made every effort not to be alone with him again during the rest of their honeymoon.

And now they were nearly home. The helicopter that had transported them from SeaTac to the hotel landed smoothly and Galen assisted Peyton and Ellie off the aircraft. A porter from the resort came forward with a luggage rail to relay their cases to his apartment.

"Home sweet home!" Ellie said as they entered the private apartment at the top of the residence wing of the hotel.

"Speaking of home, I've contacted an agent to give us a private viewing of a few places tomorrow. You both up for that?"

He'd taken the liberty of organizing it without consulting Peyton or Ellie. He knew Ellie would be excited to check out potential new homes but he hadn't wanted to give Peyton time to find an excuse not to come with them. Telling her about their appointment tomorrow in front of Ellie, where she could scarcely say she was unavailable, was probably underhanded, but he was determined to get her input on the subject.

"Yippee!" Ellie said. "What time?"

"First thing, so make sure you get plenty of sleep

and are up early tomorrow. It shouldn't be a problem with the time difference between Hawaii and here. In fact, you'll feel like you're sleeping in."

His gaze clashed with Peyton's. She didn't look impressed. The moment Ellie was out of the room she started in.

"I won't be coming with you. I have work to do now that we're back. I'm behind on my project."

"Surely, you can spend a few hours with us. It's the weekend, after all. Can't you get back to work on Monday, like regular people?"

"Galen, I'm self-employed. My hours are my own and sometimes that means I work on the weekends."

"So tell yourself you need the time off. This is important for us—as a family."

He let the last three words hang on the air between them, saying nothing more. She shifted uncomfortably before responding.

"Fine, but don't expect me to enjoy it."

"And why wouldn't you? Doesn't every woman want to create a home?"

"I can't believe you actually said that."

He shrugged. "Hey, I'm not being deliberately sexist here. I want to create a home, too. I just think it's important that if we're going to create one together, we all need to have some input on the subject, okay?"

"Whatever," she said, completely unimpressed. "Where am I staying? Does this apartment of yours boast more than two bedrooms?"

"Luckily, it does. You can take the master, though. I can sleep in the guest bedroom. I impressed upon the agent that we needed to look at houses that were ready for immediate, or near-immediate, occupancy."

"Then it won't matter if I take the guest room, will it?"

He looked at her, prepared to argue the point, then decided that he needed to pick and choose his battles if he was going to get past that solid wall of ice she'd erected between them since the night on the beach. His hands tingled at the memory of touching her the way he had. He'd been so lost in the moment, lost in her, that when she'd shoved him away he'd been slow to react. Certainly too slow to persuade her not to run away from him again.

"If that's what you want. By the way, remember the welcome home party tonight."

Would she attempt to find an excuse to skip that, too?

"Ah, yes. That."

"You don't sound thrilled. Some of the family is flying in specially for it."

"Well, they needn't have on my behalf. To be honest, it's a bit over-the-top, isn't it?" She sounded irritated as she began to pace the room. "They only just saw us a week ago."

"And they want to share in the joy that we're married."

"Your grandmother only wants to make sure she hasn't made a mistake matching us."

"You don't seem too fond of Nagy. Why's that?"

"I don't even know her."

Peyton crossed her arms and planted her feet in

what he took as a more aggressive blocking stance. As if to say, *You can ask me all the questions you like, but you're not getting anything out of me.* He sighed.

"Look, after this we don't need to see them all until Christmas, if you don't want to."

"If we're still together by Christmas." She lifted the handle on her suitcase and started to roll it down the hallway. "I'm assuming my room is down here?"

"Yes, third on the left. Can't miss it," he said in defeat.

Whatever had come over her that night on the beach hadn't changed. In fact, there was a bigger distance between them than on the day they'd met and married. He shook his head and walked over to check his phone messages. He didn't know what had come between them but he had to get past it.

He didn't want Ellie to be disadvantaged by his decision to find a partner the way he had. The last thing he'd wanted to do was parade a string of girlfriends by her while he searched for a suitable wife, which was why he'd used Match Made in Marriage in the first place. Nagy's hit rate had been 100 percent—pretty damn impressive in this day and age. She didn't make mistakes.

So why did Peyton already want out? Obviously, she didn't think they stood a chance. But why wasn't she prepared to at least try? Maybe he'd moved too fast while they were in Hawaii, but she'd been the one to put the moves on him that night. He'd held himself back until he could hold back no further. And he knew she'd been as invested in their lovemaking as he. More, in fact. The sounds she'd made, her physical responses… All of it had driven him to near madness. He groaned out loud in frustration. For the first time in his life he'd found the one woman he couldn't charm, and he didn't like it one little bit.

"At least try to look as if you're enjoying yourself," Galen whispered in her ear as she stood to one side surveying the room full of Horvaths.

A small gathering, he'd said. She growled internally. There were at least twenty-five people here, all of them close relatives of his. Ellie was in her element, showing off her tan and telling everyone who'd listen about swimming and pony riding and her new friend she'd made. It seemed she knew and loved everyone at the party and that those feelings were strongly returned.

"I'm enjoying myself," she retorted.

"Then would it kill you to smile a little?"

"Like this?" She bared her teeth at him.

"Well, I guess that's better than looking like you'd like to barbecue us all on the nearest spit. You know you could have invited your family, too. This wasn't supposed to be a one-sided thing."

"My father was otherwise occupied," she answered.

Or at least he probably would have been if she'd even told him about this.

"Look," she continued, "I'm just tired and cranky. Go, enjoy the crowd. I'll be fine here for now."

"Are you sure? You're not going to run out on me, are you?"

"Of course not. Go, please."

She felt her body sag with relief when he did what she said. The past couple of days had been a trial. While she'd determinedly kept away from him, her body tormented her by being on high and hopeful alert for whenever he was near. It left her exhausted during the day, and then at night, a recurrent dream of being on the beach with him, of finishing what they'd started, plagued her. Every darn time she had the dream, she woke hovering on the edge of orgasm and feeling as unfulfilled and frustrated as it was possible to feel. This morning she'd given in and brought herself to climax, but while the physical stimulation had brought her release, it certainly hadn't brought her satisfaction. If anything, it had only left her even more aware of Galen's proximity and of how often he brushed by her with a casual touch that seemed to leave him unaffected but reduced her to a taut set of jangling nerves every time.

Ten

Alice watched the newlyweds. All was not well in the state of Washington if their body language was anything to go by. Again, she felt that frisson of foreboding that had struck her before their wedding. Something wasn't right, but they couldn't give up. She detached herself from the group she'd been talking to and made a beeline for Peyton, who submitted to Alice's kiss on the cheek.

"Mrs. Horvath," she said in acknowledgment.

"I thought we'd discussed this before, my dear. Call me Alice, or Nagy. We're family, remember."

"Of course," she replied with a smile that was more caricature than genuine.

"If you don't mind me saying so, you're hardly the

picture of a blooming bride. What's wrong?" Alice asked bluntly.

"Wrong? Why should anything be wrong?" Peyton hedged.

"Based on our analysis of your suitability to be matched with my grandson, absolutely nothing. However, it's clear that you're not happy. What is it?"

While Alice knew Peyton was hardly likely to tell her the real reason why she was so out of sorts, she couldn't help but ask. She watched as the girl shifted her gaze and sought Galen across the room. He lifted his eyes and met hers. Peyton visibly stiffened and a bloom of color filled her cheeks. Good, Alice thought. There was a connection between them. There was hope this would still work out.

"I guess it's hard to put into words," Peyton finally admitted.

"Of course it is, dear. Look, do you mind if we take a seat over there? My stamina isn't what it used to be."

"Sure."

Alice led the way to a group of chairs and sat down heavily in the nearest one. "I'm not as spry as I used to be," she said as Peyton settled down opposite her. "Now, tell me what's wrong."

"Nothing you can help with, I'm sure."

"I have a fair bit of experience behind me, my dear. Try me and see."

"Look, I'd rather not talk about me. Can we talk about you instead?"

"Me?" Alice feigned surprise.

"Yes, you. You're fascinating. You built a successful

business into an empire. That's not a feat many women get the opportunity to achieve." Peyton was full of admiration but to Alice's ear it sounded forced. "I imagine you made some tough decisions along the way."

"I worked hard and I made sure that I never lost contact with the heartbeat of the business. Every department reported to me personally. Plus, I made sure I had the right people in those departments. Those that weren't right, left. Thankfully, there were only a few."

She watched as Peyton chewed over her words for a moment.

"You must have made some enemies along the way."

"One or two. No one ever reaches the top of their field without upsetting a few apple carts. There are some things I regret and they weigh on me now that I'm older, but I stand by my decisions." She met Peyton's gaze head-on.

"You'd retired from Horvath Corporation. What led you to establish Match Made in Marriage? Was it a financial decision or did you do it just out of boredom?"

Alice laughed out loud. She adored how blunt Peyton was. "Oh, my dear, you are priceless. I have to admit, I admire your forthright nature. It reminds me of myself, actually. In answer to your question, once I retired from Horvath Corporation I found I lacked a challenge. Since so many of the couples I'd introduced over the years went on to form lasting partnerships, I decided I may as well enlist the help of some experts and make it official.

"It's not every dating agency that can boast a one hundred percent success rate. I don't hold with these modern notions of dating apps and swiping left and right based on a few words and a photo. It takes strength and fortitude to build a marriage, together with like-minded thinking and a fair amount of physical attraction. My grandson is a handsome man, yes?"

"Oh, yes," Peyton agreed automatically. "When you say one hundred percent success rate, are you basing that on couples who have continued to stay together for years, or merely on couples who have survived the three-month minimum marriage period?"

"Continued to stay together for years, of course." Alice contemplated Peyton seriously. "It's a wonderful thing, you know, to find someone's perfect match. I was thrilled when your profile came across my desk. I knew you were perfect for Galen, and he for you. And Ellie?" Alice nodded across the room. "Well, she's just the icing on the cake for you both. Such a delightful child—I love her dearly. A family isn't only about those born into it, Peyton. It's about everyone."

After a little more small talk Peyton excused herself. Alice stayed where she was, watching her walk away. Had she done enough? she wondered. Or was it already too little, too late?

"I think I'll stay home today," Peyton said at breakfast the next morning.

"Don't you like us anymore?" Ellie asked quietly from across the table.

Galen watched for Peyton's response.

"Of course I like you," Peyton protested.

"You're acting different since we're back," Ellie persisted.

"That's because now that we're back, I need to return to work. Life isn't a perpetual holiday, you know."

"What's *perpetual* mean?"

Galen interceded before Peyton could respond. "It's something that's never-ending. How about you look it up in your dictionary and see if you can use it in a sentence when you get back to school tomorrow?"

"Good idea," Ellie said and, fired with purpose, she pushed away from the table and went to her room.

Galen took her seat and turned it to face Peyton.

"Your opinion is important. It's going to be home to all three of us, so of course we need your input. Please come."

He watched as she waged some internal battle.

"Fine, I'll come," she grumbled.

They both rose from their seats at the same time, bumping into one another. Galen put out his hands to steady her and she looked up at him. He saw confusion in her eyes and then a flare of something else— quickly masked as she pulled away. He let his hands drop down to his sides, wondering why she was so determined to continue creating as much distance between them as possible.

"Peyton, what have I done to upset you?"

"Upset me? You haven't upset me," she said, taking another step away.

"Really? Because it feels like you can't stand to be

in the same space as me anymore and, to be honest, I thought we were making progress."

She looked startled but at least she didn't leave the room immediately.

"Progress?" She spoke the word as if she was feeling it on her tongue, as if it was a foreign concept to her. "Correct me if I'm wrong, but you married to create a more stable home environment for Ellie, did you not?"

"I did," he agreed.

"And you said you weren't looking for the heights of passion or anything like that."

"I may have said words to that effect, but that doesn't mean that given the clear attraction between us we can't make something of that and build on it."

"To be honest, Galen, I don't think it's a good idea. It'll send a confusing message to Ellie if she sees us embarking on a romantic relationship when we barely know each other."

Galen wanted to argue but he could see she had a point. "Yes, that's true, but she took delight in us kissing a couple of days ago. To her it's normal to see the people who care for her care for each other, too."

"I can't believe you're using that to try to get me into bed."

Peyton's words hit him like a bucket load of icy-cold water. "You're accusing me of using her?"

She stared back at him for a moment before answering. "Well, aren't you?"

"Look, you're taking this out of context. Yes, all I wanted was an uncomplicated union with a like-minded individual. Match Made in Marriage promised me that. I was unexpectedly delighted to meet you and marry you." He paused, unsure whether it was a good idea to lay his cards on the table now, or to hold them close to his chest. He opted for the former. "I won't lie, Peyton. I'm so fiercely attracted to you that I can barely think straight. That night, on the beach, that was magical. Yes, I can understand we probably moved too quickly for your liking. I get that you don't want to race into that side of marriage, but at least give a man some hope for the future. If we were matched it was because we had similar interests, similar likes and dislikes. Please don't tell me that I'm wrong, that we have nothing in common, or that you don't find me attractive, too, because I can't believe that."

Peyton had grown pale during his speech.

"Are we ready to go?" Ellie said as she bounded back into the room.

"I just need to get my bag," Peyton said, leaving the room as quickly as humanly possible without breaking into a sprint worthy of a cheetah.

"Yeah, kiddo, we're just about ready," Galen answered as Ellie looked from Peyton's retreating back to his face.

"You talked her into coming, didn't you?" the nine-year-old said, beaming at him with great pleasure.

"Looks like it."

The apartment phone started to ring and he answered it. The real-estate agent had arrived, ready to escort them to the properties. He'd just hung up as Peyton rejoined them. Her color was back, he noted, and she'd applied some lipstick and combed her hair, but he could see by the look in her eyes that she wasn't entirely happy to be involved in this little jaunt.

"Thank you," he said sincerely as she came to a halt.

She shrugged in response. "Let's get this over with."

Galen couldn't help but smile. "You make it sound like we're leading you to your execution. Trust me— it won't be as bad as that."

"It had better not be," she said firmly. Then, letting Ellie take her hand, she led the way out the front door.

They'd already looked at two houses, both beautiful, but both completely unsuitable for their requirements. Galen had been adamant that he didn't want Ellie to be too far from her school or her friends, and the agent assured him that the last property on the list for the day would meet their needs. When they pulled up in the driveway outside the multibay garage, Peyton began to think the woman might be right. This property looked big enough for all three of them; the bedrooms weren't too close together and they wouldn't be bumping into one another all the time, like they seemed to do in the apartment. Here, Peyton could definitely have her space while she finished her article. Better yet, the property was vacant and ready for immediate occupation and had a stunning view over Puget Sound.

She couldn't believe how quickly things went after

that—after a few phone calls they were told they could take possession the following weekend.

"I can arrange a truck to collect your things for you," Galen offered as they drove back to his apartment.

"No, that's okay. I thought I'd keep my apartment for now."

He shot her a glance before putting his attention back on the road, and she noticed his hands tighten ever so much on the wheel. To her relief, he didn't raise the subject again during their ride home.

But once Ellie went to bed that night and before she could escape to her own room, he asked her to join him for a nightcap. She was on the verge of saying no, but he preempted her by pouring two snifters of brandy and gesturing toward the sofa where he'd been sitting earlier. Feeling trapped, she took the glass he'd poured and chose one of the easy chairs opposite the sofa.

"What is it?" she said, coming straight to the point.

"You never mentioned you were keeping your apartment."

"Look, it's still early days—you can't blame a girl for being a little cautious."

"Peyton, we're married. That takes a level of commitment I'm not seeing from you."

"Wow, talk about making me feel like I've just been sent to the principal's office," she said, trying to lighten the mood.

But he was right. She wasn't as committed because she *was* using him. So how did she play this? It was becoming harder to stay focused when every time she was alone with him, all she could think about was how his mouth had felt on hers. The taste of him, the feel of him beneath her hands. She was shaken by the swell of sheer need that bloomed from deep inside her and knew if she allowed herself to capitulate at that final barrier and let him make love to her, let herself make love to him, she'd never be able to complete this task she'd set for herself.

She decided to approach their conversation from another angle. Perhaps a blend of honesty, a few select words about her past and an appeal to his chivalry would get her out of this awkward mess.

"Look, Galen, I've avoided commitment for a long time because of a really traumatic experience in my past. I—" She paused, partly for effect but also because of the massive lump that suddenly appeared in her throat. "I loved someone very much once. Losing them broke me apart. I don't know if I'm actually capable of feeling that level of love for another person again."

He leaned forward, concern painted clearly in his beautiful eyes. For a moment Peyton felt a shaft of guilt. He was only trying to do the right thing and she, most definitely, was not.

"Can we at least try?" he asked. "It's clear we're attracted to each other. You chose to get into this with me. No one forced your hand. You had to know that intimacy would come up at some stage."

"But not this soon!" she blurted without thinking.

"I don't want to put myself at risk of being hurt like that again. Please respect that."

"So you want all the appearances of a good marriage, without the trimmings?"

A crooked smile pulled at his lips and she felt that all-too-familiar tug deep inside. He was so easy to fall for, so easy to want to get to know, so easy to *want*, period.

"Isn't that what you wanted, too?" she asked, remembering his words during their wedding reception.

He sighed and sat back again, his hands now resting on the tops of his thighs, fingers splayed. Somehow, she couldn't take her eyes off them. Couldn't stop herself remembering their gentle, sensual touch on her skin.

"It's what I thought I wanted but here we are, just over a week out and, to be totally honest with you, I want more."

Peyton lifted her gaze to his face, to the entreaty in his eyes.

"I can't give you more. Not yet."

Even as she said the words she felt guilt slice through her. If the circumstances had been different then, yes, maybe she would have grasped what he was offering her with both hands and run with it. But they weren't. It was as simple as that.

"Well, I guess I have to thank you for your honesty and hope that at some stage your feelings about the matter will change. It won't, however, change how I feel about you."

She nodded and took a sip of the brandy. It warmed

a trail down her throat. "Your own feelings about me might change, too," she said, mindful of how he would probably react when he discovered her true reason for marrying him.

She doubted he'd be quite as keen on making theirs a real marriage in every sense when that happened. In fact, she doubted he'd even be able to stand the sight of her anymore. That knowledge seared into her heart like a burning arrow but she forced herself to ignore the sensation. People hurt people. She'd been on the receiving end of it often enough to know she didn't want to go through that ever again.

"I need an early night. Thanks for the drink."

But as she stood and took her glass through to the kitchen, leaving Galen in the semi-dark of the lounge room, she couldn't help but acknowledge that somehow he'd wended his way through the labyrinthine corridors that protected her emotions and that when she did walk away from him, it would hurt her, too.

Eleven

"But I don't want to go. Why do I have to?"

Peyton heard Ellie's vehement words as she made her way downstairs to breakfast. They'd been in the house a week and each morning had presented some drama or another as they settled into a new routine.

"It's to earn your next Girl Scout achievement, isn't it?" was Galen's response. "Besides, all your friends are going. You don't want to be left out while they're away having a great time. It's just one night, Ellie, and you love the museum."

"I'm not going," Ellie said again, just as forcefully as the first time.

"Oh, yes, you are, young lady," Galen responded with equal determination.

Peyton walked into the breakfast room just as Ellie's lower lip began to wobble.

"Hey, guys. What's going on?"

"Galen says I have to go but I don't and I'm not going to," Ellie said with a tremor in her voice.

"She does and she will," Galen said, sounding more adamant than Peyton had ever heard him.

"Whoa, take a breath, everyone, will you?" Peyton said, holding her hands up for further effect. "First, Ellie, tell me what this is about."

Peyton gave Galen a stern look, warning him to stay quiet, as Ellie began to tell her about the overnight camp at the museum.

"That sounds really fun. Why don't you want to go?" she coaxed.

"What if something happens to you?"

"Happens? Like what?" Even though she asked, she had a feeling she knew exactly where this was going.

"Like, y'know."

Ellie's shoulders slumped and a tear trickled down her face. Peyton squatted down and took her hands in hers.

"Like what happened to your mom and dad?" she asked, confronting the giant elephant in the room.

Ellie nodded. Peyton pulled her into her arms.

"Oh, honey, I can see why you're afraid. Would it help if I tell you that Galen and I will do everything we can to look after each other while you're away? Maybe we can speak with your Scout leaders and see if they'll let you call us at bedtime. Would that help?"

"Maybe."

Peyton looked up at Galen, who nodded. "I'll call

them right now, okay, Ellie?" he said, sliding his phone from his pocket.

He left the room and Peyton could hear the low tones of his voice as he made the call. She realized she was still hugging Ellie to her, and realized, too, that while she'd avoided being overly affectionate with the little girl, it somehow felt right to hold her like this—to be the one offering her comfort when she most needed it.

She wondered if whoever had adopted her little girl comforted her like this when she was distressed. Most of the time, Peyton barely allowed herself to think of the daughter she'd signed over to the private adoption agency. It simply hurt too much. But somehow, holding Ellie like this filled a hole inside her that she hadn't even wanted to acknowledge was there.

She gave the little girl one last squeeze then let her go. Offering Ellie comfort was one thing. Taking it for herself was quite another and she couldn't allow herself to fall into that trap. She'd spent most of her adult life avoiding people with children because she hadn't wanted to suffer the questions she knew it would raise in her mind. Questions about her own child's growth and development. Questions about the sound of her voice, the color of her hair, whether she was sporty or bookish or both.

Peyton couldn't help herself. She reached out to smooth back a lock of hair that had fallen forward on Ellie's face.

"Okay, we have a meeting after school with one of the leaders who will be on the trip with you," Galen said as he reentered the room. "We'll work out a management strategy together, okay?"

Ellie looked confused. "Management what?"

Peyton brushed the girl's cheek. Now that she'd allowed herself to comfort her, she simply couldn't seem to stop. "Don't worry, Ellie. It just means we're going to get together to discuss making you feel safe and secure on the trip. Honestly, we'd hate you to miss out on something that we know you're going to love."

"And if I still don't want to go?"

"We'll cross that bridge when we get there, okay? Let's not make any decisions right now," Peyton reassured her.

"Okay, kiddo. Get your bag. The bus will be at the end of the driveway in a few minutes," Galen said, gently coaxing Ellie along.

Ellie grabbed her bag and started out the breakfast room but stopped, turned and raced back to Peyton. Wrapping her arms around Peyton's neck, she whispered in her ear, "I love you."

Before Peyton could gather her thoughts together and answer, Ellie had let her go again and was racing out the door, with Galen close behind her. It was part of their morning ritual, waiting for the bus together, and to be honest, Peyton was now glad of the moment to herself to gather her thoughts together.

Ellie *loved* her? Did a child fall in love with an adult that fast or were her words merely an expression of thankfulness for bringing the argument she'd been having with Galen to a close and pushing him to find a new solution? Whatever it was, it terrified her. She wasn't here to be Ellie's mom. In truth, she wasn't here to be Galen's wife, either. And what she had planned to do would hurt them both. What was she going to do?

A week later they gathered with all the parents to bid farewell to the bus as the kids loaded aboard. Galen rested his arm across Peyton's shoulders and he was glad that, for once, she didn't pull away. And, judging by the glimpse of tears he'd seen in her eyes as Ellie had turned on the bus steps and waved to them, his wife wasn't quite as unmoved by this moment as she'd tried to portray. It was a side of her he hadn't expected to see. Peyton was normally so contained when it came to her emotions. The only time he'd seen her lose her iron grip on her control was that night during their honeymoon. Right now, however, she looked as vulnerable as any parent sending their kid away to an overnight camp.

"She'll be fine," he murmured in her ear as the bus started up and the windows were filled with young faces and waving hands.

"I know."

"I was thinking—maybe we could go out for a drive together today and have lunch somewhere."

He didn't realize quite how much he was hoping she'd say yes, until she pulled away from him.

"That sounds like a nice idea, but I have some calls to make."

She'd had a private line installed to her office at the house and she'd been spending a whole lot of time in there. He respected anyone with a strong work ethic, but he had the suspicion that a good part of her office hours were spent very determinedly staying out of his way.

Galen nodded. This was obviously a battle for another day. "Okay, maybe another time, then."

She visibly relaxed, showing she'd obviously expected him to push back.

"Yeah, sure, another time."

"I'll drop you back home then head into the office for a while."

"Thanks."

He cringed internally. Things between them were so damn stilted. He hated it. They walked together to the car. Together, yes, but apart, as well. No touching, no accidental brushing of their bodies. *It'll work out*, he encouraged himself. *It's still early days*. They'd only been married a month; they were still getting to know one another. But even as he gave himself the little pep talk, he knew the problems went deeper. Peyton was deliberately shielding herself from him. Was it really because of her long-lost love, or was it something more?

After dropping her home and getting to Horvath Hotels and Resorts head office, he settled himself at his desk and tried to turn his attention to work. It was hopeless. All he could think about was Peyton and how little he knew about her. There was someone who could help with this, he realized—his grandmother. Did he want to ask her advice on the situation, or should he turn to his brother or cousin Ilya instead?

Or did he simply try to work this out himself? He twiddled his pen end over end between his fingers before slapping it onto his desk with a hard smack. He had to do this himself. Running to anyone else when he had a problem wasn't his style. He solved problems, period.

So, he and Peyton didn't know each other that well yet. She'd opened up a little when he'd cooked her a meal in Hawaii. Maybe he'd try that tactic again tonight and see where it led. He'd noticed that when she was working she was oblivious to the world around her, even to the point of needing to be reminded to have meals. She wouldn't even notice him coming home and cooking for her. But he might need a little help preparing for the meal.

He picked up the phone and called the new housekeeper. Peyton had been adamant she didn't want live-in staff in the house, so they'd compromised. Galen had hired a woman who was happy to come six days a week to do cleaning and some meals along with supervising Ellie after school as necessary.

When Maggie answered the phone he told her what he had in mind. She was more than happy to do the shopping for him and told him everything would be waiting in the fridge when he got home. He hung up satisfied that he finally had a plan in action.

Galen made it home early and went upstairs to change, noting that Peyton's office door was firmly closed—a good indicator that she was in the zone and working hard. Once he'd changed into jeans and a T-shirt he went down to the kitchen and opened the refrigerator. As good as her word, Maggie had made sure everything he'd asked for was there. He took out the butterflied chicken and prepared a honey-and-rosemary marinade to paint it with. Once he'd done that and added some seasoning, he took the bird in its dish outside and set it in the barbecue to roast. He quickly scrubbed some baby potatoes and put them in a pot, ready to cook. Then he set to dicing zucchini, mushrooms, onions and bell peppers, and pushed them onto metal skewers ready to add to the barbecue before the chicken was done.

Preparing their meal was wonderfully relaxing. He'd never really been one to just sit, preferring active relaxation instead. As a kid his parents had teased him for having ants in his pants, but no matter how much people urged him to stop and smell the roses he'd always needed to be doing something, anything, to feel good. And he felt good now. Anticipation thrummed a steady beat through his veins as he set the table, adding some flowers from the garden and a couple of squat white candles set on colored sand in glass bowls. He'd always had a certain flair for setting the tone of a room—it was something that had stood him in good stead as he'd climbed through the ranks at Horvath Hotels and Resorts.

Thinking about those years reminded him of his friends Nick and Sarah. A few years older than he was, they'd been quick to take him under their respective wings and show him the ropes here at the offices and resort in Port Ludlow. When he'd assumed the top role as CEO of the chain, they'd been as supportive of him then as they had back in the early days. He missed them every single day. Bestowing him with the responsibility of raising their daughter had been a gift he accepted with an immense sense of sadness and duty blended with a whole lot of love.

Despite appearances, he wasn't as free with his feelings and emotions as people thought. Yes, he had always been that good-time guy who made everyone around him laugh and made everything feel like a party. But overall he was rarely deeply invested in another human being to the extent that he was with his family, or with Ellie and her parents.

And now there was Peyton. He'd thought he could go into marriage keeping things light. How wrong could a man be? Yes, he'd wondered if Peyton's constant pushback wasn't just making him want to try harder simply because he wasn't used to not getting his way. But when he considered it fully, he realized he'd been an idiot to think he could have a marriage without emotions getting complicated. Life was complicated. Their union no less so. And while he'd specified companionship over love everlasting on his application, and assumed she also must have for them to be matched, he now knew that wasn't enough. Nor would it ever be.

Deep in thought, he went down to the wine cellar and chose a bottle of wine to enjoy with dinner. He'd noticed Peyton had a preference for oaked chardonnay and he knew he had a particularly nice one from New Zealand in his collection. After finding the bottle he went back upstairs, surprised to find Peyton poking around the kitchen.

"Something smelled good, so I had to come downstairs and see what's cooking."

He smiled in response. Her office window was above the outdoor grill. There had been an ulterior motive behind his decision to cook the chicken outdoors.

"Did you have lunch?" he asked.

"Lunch? What's that?" she answered lightly.

"You don't take very good care of yourself, do you?"

"I do okay."

"Well, you'll be pleased to know I do more than okay in the kitchen."

He grabbed a large round wooden board from under the kitchen bench then went to the fridge and gathered up some tempting goodies to tide them over until dinner was ready. The Brie Maggie had bought at the store was perfectly ripe and Galen added some sun-dried tomatoes, olives and stuffed baby bell peppers to the board along with a few slivers of fresh French bread.

"That looks like a meal in itself," Peyton said, grabbing one of the peppers and popping it into her mouth.

"Just an appetizer. Shall we take it outside?"

"Can I carry anything for you?" she offered.

"How about you bring the wine and glasses."

He went and checked the chicken after putting the wooden board on the outdoor table. Peyton sat down and poured them each a glass of wine. He rejoined her, making a point to sit right next to her so they were both facing out to the Sound.

"To us," he said, lifting his glass toward hers.

"Yes…to us."

She didn't wholeheartedly join him in the toast but she made it. He'd take that as a win, he decided.

"Did you get a lot of work done today?"

She nodded. "I've spent most of the afternoon compiling my research. The actual writing comes next."

"I imagine it's difficult to decide on what you're going to use and what you need to leave out."

"Yeah, it can be. Especially when the subject is very close to your heart."

She helped herself to a piece of bread and spread some Brie on it. He watched as she bit into it and felt his whole body grow taut as she groaned in appreciation.

"This is so good. Try some."

And just like that, she turned the conversation in another direction. He'd let her, for now, but sooner or later Peyton would begin to open up to him and he'd be right here to listen when she did.

By the time dinner was cooked and they went inside to the dining room to eat, he knew she was beginning to relax. Maybe it was the wine, or maybe it had been the morsels of food she'd picked at before dinner, but he sensed she had lowered her barriers a little.

After dinner they retired to the sitting room. It was a beautiful space, with a wooden cathedral ceiling and tall glass sliding doors that opened out onto the deck. The views of the Sound were spectacular. This had been one of the main features of the property that had made him want to buy it, and he'd come to look forward to relaxing in here in the evenings to unwind after work. It was all the better for Peyton's company tonight.

She sank onto the overstuffed sofa with a sigh of contentment.

"That was a truly beautiful meal. Thank you."

"My pleasure."

They lapsed into a companionable silence. Galen topped up their wineglasses and handed Peyton hers.

"It's quiet without Ellie," she commented.

"You're a natural with her. From helping her overcome her fear of the sleepover, to seeing her off today. You did great."

Peyton's face froze for a moment, but then she smiled. He watched her, realizing that when she smiled, there was no joy behind it.

"I'm glad you think so. Despite the fact you haven't been her father all her life, you do a great job, too—you make it look so effortless." She sighed and pulled her feet up underneath her on the sofa. "Parenthood doesn't come naturally to me."

Galen sensed she had a lot more to say, but was just finding the right words. Rather than prompt her, he maintained his silence and watched the emotions that played over her face. She drew in another deep breath and let it go slowly as if she was gearing up for something really important. He felt his whole body tense in anticipation.

"I—" The word came out as a croak and Peyton cleared her throat before starting again. "I had a baby once. I gave her away."

Twelve

Her heart hammered in her chest. There, she'd said the words out loud. The secret she'd never disclosed to anyone other than her dad and those immediately involved in the birth and subsequent adoption of her little girl. To his credit, Galen didn't look as shocked as she thought he might. When he spoke, his voice was incredibly gentle.

"How long ago?"

"Nearly ten years."

"So your baby would be Ellie's age now?" He caught on quickly. "That's got to be difficult for you. I had no idea."

"Well, I didn't exactly include the information in my application," she said, trying to make light of it. "It's not something I like to talk about."

But the lump in her throat grew thicker and she swallowed hard against it, worried she might do the unthinkable and actually cry in front of Galen. She always fought to keep her emotions in check. Life was messy enough without them. But right now it was more difficult than usual.

"She was absolutely perfect," Peyton managed to say, allowing herself a brief moment to remember the rosebud lips, the soft downy blond hair and the sweet scent of her child.

"And her dad? Was he supportive?"

"He was dead."

"Did he know about the baby?"

She shook her head. "He was a marine. He died on his first deployment. Not active duty—a car accident. I didn't find out until quite a while after. I thought, when I contacted him to tell him I was pregnant, that maybe he was just ghosting me. Y'know, it was a good time while it lasted but now it's over kind of thing."

She saw she had shocked him. He rose from his seat and joined her on the sofa. "Peyton, I'm so sorry. Did you have any help from home?"

"My mom died when I was in junior high. My dad, well…"

She let her voice trail away. How did she describe her dad? Bitter. Angry. Resentful. He had told her she could sort out her own problems.

Peyton didn't notice the point at which Galen had taken her hand, but right now his warm, steady grip was grounding, something she could focus on rather than the words that tumbled from her.

"It was hell. I was still in college, nearing the end of my degree. I didn't know what to do or where to turn. A few weeks before she was born I finally accepted that no matter what happened, I couldn't keep her. I just couldn't offer her the opportunities she deserved. I looked into adoption and through a counselor I received additional information about private adoption. I went for that in the end."

She didn't mention how choosing to go with that option had made her feel as though she'd been a womb for hire. As if her baby was a commodity to buy and sell, and not a living, breathing human being. But she'd still have been paying off her student loans now if she hadn't agreed to her costs being covered by the adopting family.

"Do they share information with you about your daughter?"

She shook her head. "No. I wanted it that way. I didn't think it was fair to give her away and expect to still be a part of her life."

"And if she wants to find you one day?"

Peyton shrugged. "The option is open to her. Her adoptive family insisted on it."

"They sound like decent people."

"I certainly hope they are, and that she's happy."

Her voice broke on the last word and she closed her eyes, not wanting to give in to the feelings that threatened to swamp her. There was a reason she'd kept everything locked deep down inside and that reason was self-preservation. If she'd allowed herself the luxury of indulging in her emotions then the memories would rise up and swallow her, much as they appeared to want to do now. It was too much. She needed a distraction.

"Galen?"

"Hmm?"

"Would you make love to me?"

She felt shock ripple through him, his fingers tightening on her hand in a grip that was almost painful.

"Are you sure about this, Peyton?"

She shifted on the sofa so she was facing him, so his mouth was only a hairbreadth from hers.

"Yes," she whispered.

Then she leaned forward and kissed him. She didn't want any more words. Words only reawakened the pain and sorrow she'd pushed so deep down inside. Now she wanted actions, feelings, sensation. Anything and everything so she could just stop hurting again.

His lips were smooth and supple against hers and she wasted no time, rising onto her knees and straddling his lap. She held his head and angled her face so she could kiss him more deeply and felt his body's answering heat and desire flame to life beneath her. Then his hands were on hers, holding them away from him, and he pulled away slightly.

"What is it? Don't you want this?" she asked, breathless with the desire that pulsed through her.

"Oh, I want this. I want to be certain you do, too. This isn't a one-shot deal, Peyton. As much as I want to let you use me to push away your past, I can't just make love with you and then go back to where we were this morning."

He was asking for her commitment. It was only reasonable. When it came to her, the man was so fiercely astute it was frightening. But right now her body and her mind clamored for the relief she knew being with him would bring. She didn't want to think past this moment. And the idea of commitment? It was too much. But he needed a response and she owed it to him.

"I understand," she forced herself to say.

She'd deal with the outcome of tonight's choice later. Right now she wanted him and she wanted oblivion, in that order. She kissed him again, shifting her pelvis this time so her body ground against his, letting him know how much she wanted him.

"You're not being fair, Peyton," he said against her lips. "You're tormenting me. In fact, you've been a torment since the first time I laid eyes on you."

"Then let's ease our torment together. Let's go upstairs."

She wriggled off his lap and stood in front of him, holding out her hand. She'd made the invitation; it was up to him to accept it. Whatever came next was all down to him. He didn't hesitate. He took her hand and rose to his feet, then led her through the room and up the stairs and along the gallery to the master suite.

"Now is the time to leave if you don't want to go any further, Peyton. I'm serious."

"Then let's not pretend," she answered, stepping closer and reaching up to stroke his face. "So solemn.

Let's see if we can't change that," she murmured before going on tiptoes and kissing him again.

"I can't think when you do that," he protested.

"And when I do this?"

She slid her hands under his T-shirt and up to his chest, where she found the flat discs of his nipples and squeezed them gently.

"And when you do that," he affirmed.

"And what about this?"

Peyton let one hand slide down his torso, to his belly, to the waistband of his jeans. His sharply indrawn breath allowed her to slip beneath the waistband and to his boxer briefs, where she stroked him through the fabric.

"Most definitely when you do that," he groaned. "In fact, pretty much when you do anything."

She gently gripped him, squeezing slightly before letting him go and pulling her hand out. "You're wearing far too many clothes for what I want to do to you."

"To me? Or with me?" he asked.

"Both, either. Does it matter?"

"It matters. When it comes to you, Peyton, everything matters."

There was something in the tone of his voice that gave her pause, made her question whether or not she was doing the right thing. But the steady thrum of her pulse and the deliciously building tension of her body told her more than anything that she was in the right place at the right time. They would find pleasure in one another, that was a given. The man lit her up like the Fourth of July when he kissed her. And when he touched her...

She didn't want to think anymore. Instead, Peyton reached for his T-shirt and tugged it over his head before letting it drop to the bedroom floor. Then her hands were at his jeans, clumsily undoing the fastenings. She shoved her fingertips under the waistband of his briefs and eased them down over his hips. He stood there in front of her, gloriously naked. She wanted to touch all of him, taste him, feel him. She drew in a shaky breath before tugging away at her own clothes. The moment she was naked she wrapped herself around him, drawing in his strength and heat. His hands spread across her back, holding her even tighter to his body.

Peyton lifted her face to his and welcomed the fierceness of his kiss, the plunder of his tongue. This was what she needed. Him. All of him. Everywhere.

They backed up to his bed and he fell back on the mattress. She straddled him again, pushing his shoulders down until he was flat on the bed. Her hands molded the muscles of his shoulders as she bent her head to his throat and kissed a wet trail down the strong column and farther, to his chest. Her nostrils flared at the scent of him: heat and spice together with the fresh scent of the sea. She'd never be able to smell the ocean again without her mind being filled with him. They were intrinsically combined now. She shifted a little so she could continue her trail of kisses, her fingertips tugging gently at the spear of body hair that arrowed below his belly, her lips and tongue following.

His erection strained against her, brushing her breasts as she moved lower. She took him in her hand again and slowly stroked his hot, silky skin. His flesh jerked against her palm and she tightened her hold.

"You like this?" she asked.

"I like everything you do to me," he growled in reply.

She smiled and arched a brow. "Everything?"

"Everything." His voice was adamant.

She lowered her mouth to the swollen head of his penis, her tongue darting out to flick against him. Beneath her, he shuddered.

"Especially that," he said, his voice trembling.

She stroked her hands over his strong thighs and nuzzled the base of him before licking a path along his length and taking him into her mouth. His fingers caught in her hair as she swirled her tongue around him, taking him deeper into her mouth and sucking hard. His entire body tensed and she knew he was on the verge of losing his mind when she eased the pressure of her mouth and rose above him.

She settled herself over his glistening shaft.

"I'm glad we can dispense with any interruptions," she murmured as she began to take him into her body. "We're both clean and I'm on birth control."

He groaned as she sank down on him and rocked her pelvis. "I'm glad you're glad," he teased in return, but by the tone of his voice it took every ounce of effort he had left.

She knew how he felt. Right now all she wanted to do was bounce and buck and wring her pleasure from his body. But first, she wanted to pleasure him. She started to move, her motion gentle, deep and slow. Galen lifted his hands and cupped her breasts, his fingertips playing with her nipples—at first gently, then squeezing just a little more tightly until the delicious pain of it made her internal muscles clench on an involuntary wave of pleasure so intense she thought he'd make her come, just like this.

She fought against the urge to give in; when she came, it would be with him and because she wanted to. She increased her movements, leaning her body weight onto his upstretched arms as she got faster, and faster still. His eyes remained locked on hers, staring into her as if he could see past all her walls and into her very soul. And then she felt him buck beneath her, his climax rocketing through him, his body straining against hers, and she let go, allowing herself to disappear on the rolling crescendo of satisfaction that stole the breath from her body and the memories from her mind.

This was what she'd wanted, needed. Oblivion.

Thirteen

Making love with Peyton had been everything he'd dreamed of, and more—every single time. And yet, while they'd reached physical perfection together, there was still a disconnection between them. She'd blindsided him last night. Both with the news about the child she'd surrendered for adoption and then with their lovemaking.

He'd willingly let her take the lead, instinctively understanding that was what she needed, but while he'd made it clear that if they took that step in their relationship it meant they couldn't go back, he wondered if she hadn't simply been paying lip service to get what she needed right then.

So what happened next? He knew what he wanted out of their marriage, even if he hadn't exactly gone into it with an expectation of falling in love. But if how he was feeling right now was any indication then it was clear his expectations had done a U-turn.

Peyton shifted in the bed, her body suddenly tense.

"You okay?" he asked.

She stretched and rolled over to face him. "I'm good. And you?"

He reached out and smoothed her hair from her face, enjoying the intimacy. "I'm great. No second thoughts?"

He had to ask, needed to know what she was thinking, what she planned to do now that the cocooned world of night had been shattered by day. Peyton's eyes were slightly shadowed as she sat up abruptly, the sheets falling from her body and exposing her naked form to his hungry eyes.

She shook her head and looked back at him over her shoulder. "Not me. I'm going for a shower. Then I'll cook us a huge breakfast. I'm famished."

He smiled back, feeling the tension in both his mind and body ease. "That sounds like a great idea. Need help washing your back?"

She laughed. "If you do that, breakfast might be more like lunch."

"I can wait," he said.

He watched her as his words sank in. Her pupils dilated and her nipples tightened into dark pink buds. Buds that had felt perfect as he'd rolled them with his tongue last night. She'd been a very open lover, giving as well as receiving. Last night had been exceptional and, under other circumstances, would have left him sated. But there was something about Peyton that drove him to want more—physically and emotionally. He swung his feet to the floor, stood up and walked toward her. Her gaze roamed his body, coming to rest just below his hips.

"I see that you have something else in mind," she said with a saucy smile.

As her lips curved he felt something pull tight in his chest. Was this what love was? he wondered. This sense of being knocked sideways by something as precious as a smile? This overwhelming need to touch her and be touched by her? This wanting to know and understand her every thought? To make her happy? If it wasn't love, it was pretty darn close.

Galen held a hand out to Peyton and tugged her forward, aligning her naked body against his and relishing the heat in those areas where their bodies touched. He didn't think he could ever have enough of this, of her.

"Oh, I have a lot of things in mind right now. Every single one of them centered on you."

Her breath hitched and he saw a look of yearning on her beautiful features. A yearning that was swiftly masked by something else. She was good at that, he realized. Far too good. His wife was an expert at masking her true thoughts and feelings. In fact, the only time he thought she'd been 100 percent open and honest with him had been last night, in the sanctuary of his bed. Well, if that was what it took to get to know and understand her, then he'd gladly step up to the task.

Keeping her loved up and satisfied would be both an honor and a pleasure.

"C'mon," he said, his voice just a bit gruff. "Let's shower."

"We're going to have to hurry if we're to meet Ellie's bus," Peyton said with a laugh as she whisked eggs in a bowl.

"I can do the bacon on the outdoor grill if you like. It'll be quicker."

"Thanks. These will only take a few minutes."

"I'm onto it."

Galen snagged the packet of bacon with one hand and started to whistle as he went out onto the deck. He hadn't felt this happy in forever. Maybe it was the sense of letting go of his control over his emotions that left him feeling like he'd just been on the most incredible roller-coaster ride of his life. Whatever it was, he liked it.

He looked through the window to the kitchen and watched Peyton as she moved around. It was quite the scene of domestic bliss. Something that had been sadly lacking in the weeks prior. She'd been so wary, but then again, he had been, too. Last night, when she told him about her daughter, it had opened things up between them. But he knew she was still holding back. Peyton was complex, with multiple layers. He'd only uncovered one—a very important, deeply scarred one.

She was scarred, but strong, as well. A person would have to be, to get through that without becoming a wreck. He didn't know if, in similar circumstances, he'd have been able to face the same thing.

He thought for a minute about his female cousins. Each one of them strong and independent, benefiting from their grandmother's example. But if any one of them had faced a situation like Peyton's she'd have had a wealth of support behind her. Peyton hadn't had any of that. No wonder she was so reserved and aloof. No wonder she feared love. The more he began to understand her, the more he realized that it was fear holding her back, whether she knew it or not.

"Are you planning on burning that bacon?" Peyton called out from the kitchen, snapping him out of his reveries.

"As if I'd do such a thing," he called back and quickly snatched up a set of tongs and a plate to take the strips off the grill. "I hope you like yours crispy," he commented wryly as he reentered the kitchen.

A gurgle of laughter bubbled up from inside her, the sound making him stop in his tracks and simply drink in the joy of watching her unguarded, happy. Hell, he'd almost burn the bacon every day if it meant he could hear her laugh so honestly.

"You're lucky I do," she said, spooning a generous serving of scrambled eggs onto his plate.

"Hey, leave yourself some," he protested.

"Oh, I won't miss out, don't worry."

He looked at the clock. They had half an hour to eat and clean up before collecting Ellie at the pickup point. If only they had more time alone together. Somehow, the dynamic of having Ellie around changed things between them. He didn't regret having the little girl in his life one bit, but he suspected that sometimes being around her was like rubbing salt in the wound for Peyton. Some of the looks she'd given Ellie began to make sense now. The looks that spoke of longing and regret. Looks that were tempered with a please-don't-love-me vibe because she was too afraid to love in return. He had to break through those barriers. Somehow, he and Peyton and Ellie would become a real family.

Peyton stood with Galen's arm draped around her as they waited with the other parents for the bus to arrive. It all felt so normal and so foreign at the same time. Things had changed since they'd been here in the same spot yesterday. Then, she'd been full of trepidation for Ellie, an emotion that had been swiftly chased by pride in the girl as she'd shouldered her anxiety and climbed on board the bus.

And hadn't she done something similar herself last night? She tightened her hold on Galen's waist, taking strength in his nearness and his solid presence beside her. Was this what marriage had been like for her parents before her mom had gotten sick—before her dad had changed? The sad thing was, she couldn't even ask him. He'd been so filled with seething anger, even going so far as destroying the photo albums her mom had so patiently and lovingly made up for Peyton as a way of remembering her when she was gone.

She wondered where Ellie's parents' pictures were and made a mental note to ask Galen. While she knew that Ellie's old bedroom from her parents' home had been faithfully replicated at his apartment and then more recently in their new house, she had no idea what had happened to everything else. Maybe it would help Ellie to feel more secure and connected if she had access to more of her happy memories with her mom and dad.

And when you move on, what then? Her conscience pricked sharply.

Beneath her hand, she felt Galen's body tense.

"There's the bus," he exclaimed. "And there she is!"

With his free hand he began waving madly. Peyton felt her heart constrict. They had been very occupied during Ellie's absence, but it was clear Galen hadn't stopped worrying about her.

The next half hour was filled with a blur of retrieving the overnight bags and girls saying goodbye to each other until, finally, they were able to climb into the car and get back to the house.

"You had a good time?" Galen asked after Ellie did up her seat belt.

"I had the best time."

"So you're glad you went?" Peyton pressed.

"Yeah, thank you for making me go. It was really cool."

Their ride home was peppered with Ellie's excitement, which stretched out into the afternoon. Peyton helped her unpack and put her things in the wash, teaching her how to do each step.

"My mommy used to do this but at the hotel apartment Galen just sent our laundry out. Do I have to do this all the time now?" Ellie asked as she turned on the washer.

"If you want to. It's good to know how to take care of yourself."

"But what if I don't want to?"

"Well, you have me and we have Maggie."

"Did your mommy teach you?"

"No. My mommy got sick and wasn't able to do a lot of stuff."

"I'm sorry."

"It was a long time ago."

Ellie enveloped her in a hug. "I'm glad you're with us now. You don't need to be alone anymore."

The child's simple words cut her to her core. Alone? She felt like she'd spent her entire life alone from the day of her mom's diagnosis. And now that she actually had something, she was gearing up to leave it all behind her again. She awkwardly returned Ellie's hug and then pulled away.

"C'mon, you can help me prepare a salad for dinner. Galen's grilling steaks and baking potatoes."

"Yum!"

And just like that the moment changed. Kids were so adaptable, she thought as she followed Ellie through to the kitchen. Maybe she needed to be a bit more like that.

The evening went quickly and it wasn't long before Ellie was drooping with exhaustion. After Galen had seen her to bed, Peyton went into her office to work on her article. She read through the opening paragraphs, but instead of the sense of triumph she expected, she ended up with a knot in her stomach. She sighed in frustration and dropped her head in her hands. Why was writing this so hard? She'd planned it for years, relished the opportunity to depose Alice Horvath from the heady pedestal on which everyone put her. This should be the easiest thing in the world to her. It didn't involve political upheaval; it didn't involve genocide or massive environmental damage— all of which she'd written about to great acclaim in the past. So what was wrong with her? Was it that she was too close to the subject matter? Too biased, perhaps?

No, it wasn't personal bias. She'd found others, like her father, who'd been summarily dismissed from their jobs at various Horvath Corporation branches. Locating them had been like finding needles in haystacks, and a handful had signed nondisclosure agreements on their termination, so they had politely, but firmly, rebuffed her attempts to interview them. But the others backed up her father's experience.

Peyton had always prided herself on balanced reporting. Up until now all she'd accumulated was one side of the story. And there was her answer. She needed to go straight to the source. She needed to interview Alice. Her stomach knotted in anticipation. Would the grand matriarch grant her an audience? It was well known that Alice didn't do interviews. Hey, she could ask, right? But what would be the best way to approach her?

A sound behind her made her minimize her open computer window, swivel in her chair and look at the door. Galen stood there, one arm casually propped against the frame and looking far too sexy for his own good. Her body tightened on a surge of remembrance. This afternoon had been about Ellie, but right now her mind was crammed with all the things she and Galen had done together last night.

"Everything okay?" Galen asked.

"Yes, and no," she admitted. How could she approach this? she wondered. Just ask him straight-out if his grandmother would talk to her, perhaps? But for what reason? An idea sprang to her mind. "A part of my article focuses on strong women in business. Would Alice agree to an interview, do you think?"

What she'd said wasn't a total lie. Galen straightened and took a step inside her office. He frowned a little.

"She's not a fan of interviews. You probably know that already."

"I had heard something like that," Peyton said lightly. "But there's no harm in asking her, right? If she says no, it's no." She shrugged as if it didn't matter.

Galen stroked his chin thoughtfully. "I could talk to her for you."

"No, I wouldn't ask you to do that. Using you as a go-between would be cowardly."

"You're probably right. In fact, I know you're right. Nagy would probably see it as a weakness and dismiss the idea immediately."

Peyton nodded. "I'll call her tomorrow, and just get straight to the point."

Galen moved closer and rested his hands on her

shoulders, massaging the knots of muscle that had formed there while she worked. "Good idea. What will you do if she says no?"

"Move on to the next person on my list. Alice's input isn't vital to my article, but I'd be keen on hearing her out."

"Then let's hope she's in a magnanimous mood tomorrow," he said on a chuckle. "Jeez, you're so tight. Is this what working on your articles does to you?"

"Sometimes, especially when things aren't going as well as I'd like. But y'know what?"

"What?"

"I know something that loosens me up like nothing else."

His hands stilled and she heard his sharply indrawn breath. "And that might be?"

"Oh, I think you know what I mean," she answered as she rose to her feet. "Or have you forgotten already? Perhaps I need to refresh your memory."

She entwined her arms around his neck and lifted her face to his, taking possession of his mouth in a kiss that she knew would leave him in no doubt of what she was talking about. Thankfully, he was a quick study. She felt his body's instant response to her invitation, and when he scooped her in his arms and stalked with her across the landing toward the master suite, she allowed herself to thrill in the anticipation of what she knew would come next.

Fourteen

"Thank you so much for agreeing to see me, Mrs. Horvath."

Alice forced herself to smile. "Please, dear. I've asked you already to call me Alice or Nagy. If you keep referring to me as Mrs. Horvath I'll think you're not really a part of the family."

She had kept the censure from her voice but she didn't miss the swiftly masked expression on the younger woman's face. Was it irritation, perhaps, or embarrassment? Or maybe something else? Since her operation she didn't feel quite as sharp as she used to be and it annoyed her intensely. Getting old certainly wasn't for sissies. Luckily, she'd never been a sissy in her life.

"I'm sorry, Alice," Peyton apologized.

"That's better, dear. See? It didn't hurt a bit, did it?" Alice allowed herself a small smile. "I hope you enjoyed your flight?"

"Having a company jet at my disposal isn't something I think I'll ever get used to but, yes, it was a smooth trip."

"Good. Now, please, take a seat and tell me what this article is about. It must be important to bring you all the way to California. You know I don't usually give interviews."

"Yes, I do, and I really appreciate you making time to see me."

"Time seems to be something I have a great deal more of than I wish to these days."

"Oh, isn't Match Made in Marriage keeping you busy enough?"

Alice waved a hand in front of her. "Oh, yes, that's fun. But it's hardly the cut and thrust of the corporate world, is it? And I have to say, since my surgery earlier this year, I've been forced to slow down a little. A temporary thing, I've been assured."

She firmed her lips before she said any more. She didn't like exposing her infirmities to anyone, least of all this newest member of her family. "Tell me, how is Ellie doing now that you're settling into your new home? It must have been a big adjustment for all of you—getting married and living together. But you're doing all right, I trust?"

She listened as Peyton filled her in about the little girl, nodding and smiling where necessary. She wondered if Peyton knew how her expression changed when she talked about Ellie, about the small elements of pride that shone through when she mentioned Ellie's bravery at going on the overnight visit to the museum and her latest school results. And then, how her expression became softer when she talked about Galen. Yes, Alice had made the right choice here. It had been a risk, thrusting a husband and child onto a young woman for whom career appeared to be everything, but as with so many things in life that were worthwhile, you had to take a leap of faith at some point.

Much of the tension that had been apparent on Peyton's face when they'd returned from their honeymoon had eased, but she was clearly very driven. It was a trait Alice both identified with and admired, but she knew firsthand that that drive had to be tempered or it would take over any chance for true happiness.

Peyton brought her conversation back to the point of her being there. "So, as you can see, our lives are busy. But no less busy than your life must have been with your much larger family and juggling your children's needs with the demands of the Horvath Corporation after your husband passed away."

"We women do what we do." Alice shrugged.

"That's true," Peyton agreed. "Which is what I wanted to speak with you about. I want to talk about women in business. About the balance of life and work and how that affected your decision-making."

"Affected my decision-making? You mean emotional versus rational, that sort of thing?"

Peyton looked slightly uncomfortable. "I guess, yes. We are emotional creatures, aren't we?"

"You're testing me, aren't you?" Alice said with a little laugh. "Okay, I'll give you your interview, Peyton. I respect you for both asking me directly and for coming to me, face-to-face, to conduct it. I should have expected as much from you."

"Expected as much?"

"Oh, I'm well aware of your successes in your field, young lady. I should be flattered, I suppose, that you wanted to interview me, too. That you thought my life worthy of inclusion in one of your articles. Although, I have to say, this is a shift for you, isn't it? Women in business instead of your usual David versus Goliath style of reporting?"

Peyton shifted in her chair. "Yes, it is. But you have to admit, it's a subject dear to a lot of women's hearts."

Alice smiled. It was clear that Peyton was only revealing half of her intentions. Perhaps by offering Peyton her trust, it would convince the girl that she truly was a part of the family. And if it didn't? Alice rubbed absently at her chest, a habit she still found herself indulging in even now that her heart was so much better.

If Alice had miscalculated, it might mean she'd made the first serious mistake of her life and endangered the happiness of both her much-adored grandson and the little girl he had taken responsibility for. But Alice Horvath didn't make mistakes, she reminded herself. She relaxed her features and put a smile on her face.

"Ask me your questions, my dear. And then we can enjoy lunch together and get to know each other a little better."

Peyton wondered if a butterfly caught in a net felt the same as she did right now. This interview was no different from anything she had done before, so why did she feel like a rookie reporter covering her first school event and worrying if she'd get the names right? It was ridiculous. She smiled back at Alice and took out her notepad and pen from her leather bag.

"No recorder?" Alice asked, raising one brow.

"I prefer to make notes as I go, but if you'd rather I record, I can do that using my phone."

"One of the reasons I don't usually grant interviews is because I have a deep dislike of being misquoted. At least if you have a recording, there can be no mistakes, correct?"

Peyton averted her gaze. There was something about Alice's tone that made her uncomfortable. As if she was being challenged. Or maybe it was merely her own guilt that was making it seem so. She pulled her phone from her bag, put it on the coffee table between them and selected the voice recorder app.

"There we go," she said as brightly as she could manage. "No mistakes."

"Thank you, my dear. It's good of you to indulge an old woman."

Now there was a trap laid before her if ever there

was one. Peyton couldn't help it; she laughed. "You may be older than me, Alice, but you're likely as sharp as you ever were."

She met Alice's blue eyes across the table and saw the glimmer of humor reflected there; she also noted the subtle nod of her head.

"More people would do well to remember that. Now, ask me your questions."

Peyton skimmed through what she mentally called the fluff questions, all of which appeared to bore Alice if her lackluster responses were anything to go by.

"Don't you have questions with more meat to them? I thought you wanted this article to be as hard-hitting as your usual work. Or are you targeting a new audience?" the older woman asked her with a dash of acerbity to her tone.

Peyton was a little taken aback. This was her interviewing style—fluff to soften up her subject before rounding out the interview with the serious questions that gave her the kind of answers she really wanted. The technique had served her well in the past, lulling most of her interviewees into a sense of security before she got to the point of what she wanted to know. Alice, it appeared, was not one of those people.

"No, it's not for a new audience. This will be as serious a work as anything I've done before, perhaps even more so," she replied, feeling slightly defensive.

"Then kindly get to the point."

Alice's words were delivered with a smile but Peyton was left in no doubt whatsoever that she was treading on thin ice.

"So, Match Made in Marriage. What drove you to establish the company and how successful is it, really?"

"I believe I already mentioned to you once, I have a knack for introducing people to one another. It made sense to formalize that with a company that specialized in creating introductions."

"But they're not just introductions, are they? Not when people meet for the first time at the altar," Peyton pressed.

"You approached us. You know the format."

Was that a note of censure or warning in Alice's voice? Peyton felt a tiny thrill of excitement. Was she finally getting to her? Riling up the ever-serene and much-loved Nagy, who appeared incapable of doing any wrong to her doting family.

"That's true—I did. And you delivered exactly what I asked for in my assessment questionnaire. How can you be certain, though, that every match will be a success?"

Alice narrowed her eyes a moment. "Are you speaking as a reporter now? Or from a point of fear for your own relationship with my grandson? You were unsettled when you arrived back from your honeymoon. Are things not improving?"

Peyton shook her head. Oh, the old lady was good. She'd managed to turn the tables on Peyton with next to no effort. She girded herself to take back control of the interview once more.

"We aren't talking about me and my situation. I'm

curious about the science behind the matches you make."

"It's not all science, although since I've established the company I've enlisted the assistance of psychologists and relationship experts to ensure that we're on the right track. We've had no failures so far, which is more than I can say for most dating options available to people these days. We take a lot of pride in our matches—there's a lot at stake."

"This is true," Peyton agreed. "A great deal is at stake on many levels, including the legal assurances in the agreements your clients sign. But is it true that, science and probabilities aside, you always have the final say on whether or not a couple are to be matched?"

Alice's voice had lost all its warmth when she spoke this time. "As I said earlier, I have a knack for making introductions. The science merely supports this. Our track record now speaks for itself."

"So basically, and let's be totally honest here, you're it. You're the one manipulating people's lives and potential happiness with your matches. And, despite your 'knack,' as you call it, you weren't a hundred percent on track as a younger woman, were you? After all, didn't you keep two men dangling for your attention before you chose to marry Eduard Horvath?"

Peyton knew she was taking a risk by raking up that old coal, but she wasn't here to pussyfoot around. Alice sighed and straightened her skirt over her legs.

"You didn't set this interview up to discuss Match Made in Marriage, or my past," Alice said pointedly.

"The matchmaking business is a part of who you are as a businesswoman, but if you're uncomfortable talking about Match Made in Marriage we can move on to something else. Okay, as far as I can tell, Horvath Corporation has a very high staff retention rate. But no workplace is ever perfect. Tell me about the people you've fired. Who were they, and why did you fire them?"

"Telling you who they were would be a breach of confidentiality," Alice responded smoothly.

But Peyton didn't miss the stiffening of the woman's spine.

"Without stating specifics, then. What kind of thing would lead you to release a staff member?"

"Theft and disloyalty are generally the only reasons I have been forced to let people go. And it never failed to surprise me that despite all the benefits we offered, together with very competitive salaries, there'd always be a few who thought they could dip their hands in the pot, so to speak."

"How did you deal with it?"

"How does anyone deal with theft? The consequences are clearly spelled out in staff employment agreements. The offender is terminated."

"And what process of investigation do you follow? Surely people are assumed innocent until proved guilty?"

Peyton held her breath. She still vividly remembered the day her father had come home from work, furious that he'd been dismissed without a chance to defend himself.

"The staff member is generally put on leave with full pay until an independent investigation is conducted. Depending on the outcome of that investigation, they either return to work or they go on to find work elsewhere."

"And what about the rumors I've been told, that you've interfered with some former staffers' ability to find other work?"

Alice's eyes narrowed. "I don't address rumors."

"Okay, let me rephrase that. Have you ever interfered with an ex-employee's ability to find other work in their field?"

"I believe this interview is over." Alice rose to her feet. "I look forward to seeing your article when it goes to print. Will you furnish me with an advance copy?"

And give the old lady time to file an injunction preventing its publication when she saw what the article truly held? Peyton smiled and shook her head.

"That's not my usual practice. I can't be seen to make an exception. I'm sure you understand."

"Oh, I understand, Peyton. Be careful where you tread."

"I beg your pardon?"

"I said for you to be careful where you tread. You don't know what you may inadvertently step into. Now, let's adjourn to the dining room. I believe our lunch is ready."

Peyton watched the woman as she walked slowly

and carefully across the room. The interview had left her with a bitter taste in her mouth—there were still so many questions Peyton wanted to ask. At least Alice hadn't kicked her out, but she had the feeling she'd come mighty close to it. Best not to poke the tiger any further today.

One thing, however, was crystal clear. She needed to wrap up the feature and get out of this marriage—this family—as quickly as possible.

Fifteen

Galen watched Peyton as she got ready for bed that night. There was something about her bedtime routine that he found unbelievably sexy. He rose from the bed and walked toward her where she sat at the bedroom vanity, brush in hand. He was only wearing his cotton pajama bottoms.

"Let me do that," he suggested.

She didn't protest as he took the brush from her hand and began to run it through her hair. But rather than relax her, as it usually did, she appeared to grow even more tense.

"How did the interview go with Nagy today?"

"She's the queen of stonewalling, isn't she?"

"Ah, so it didn't go well, then." He kept up the steady strokes of the brush.

"No, it didn't. Not for me, anyway. I have some quotes I can use but I didn't get near to what I really wanted."

"Do you want me to try for you? Perhaps she might be more amenable if I ask—"

"No!" Peyton blurted. "I'm sorry, but no," she repeated more gently this time. "I will work with what I have."

Galen met Peyton's gaze in the mirror. She showed obvious signs of strain around her eyes and there were shadows beneath them, too. He put down the brush and rested his hands on her shoulders.

"I only want to help you, Peyton, to make your life easier where I can."

"I know that, but you have to understand, I'm used to relying on myself. That way I have only myself to blame if something goes wrong."

"Why should anything go wrong?"

She gently shook her head and gave him a slightly pitying look. "You really have no idea, do you?"

Her words stung. Did she think he'd never known hardship or sorrow or difficulty? As if she suddenly realized how her words must have sounded, she shook her head again.

"Look, I'm sorry. Of course you know what it's like."

"Everyone has their battles to face. But you don't have to face anything alone anymore, Peyton." His fingers tightened on her shoulders and he leaned down until his face was even with hers. "I'm here for you now. All you have to do is let go and trust me to help you."

She lifted a hand to one of his, her fingers lacing in between his and squeezing them. "Thank you. It's an adjustment learning to rely on someone else. I'm not sure I'm very good at it."

"Hey, practice makes perfect, right?"

He dropped a kiss on her shoulder, then shifted her hair to expose the back of her neck and pressed his lips there. A tremor ran through her and she dropped her head forward.

"It does crazy things to me when you do that," she said softly.

"Want me to distract you some more?"

"Please."

The heartfelt plea in that single word made him want to stop and ask more about what had happened today between her and his grandmother. That it hadn't gone well had been evident in every line of her face and the way she'd carried herself when she'd arrived home a quarter of an hour ago. But now was not the time. Now was all about shifting that tiredness from her eyes and putting life and energy back in them while revitalizing her body to a point where she could forget what troubled her. She'd said she didn't want his help, but she'd accept this, so he'd give it to her.

Galen's hands slid to the straps of her nightgown and gently eased the thin strips over her shoulders and down her arms. The silky fabric of her nightie slipped down her breasts, slowly exposing them to his hungry gaze. He bent his head and kissed a line along her shoulder while his hands slid down, tugging the fabric away from her breasts completely. Her nipples had grown into taut points and the creamy flesh of her breasts rose and fell as her breathing quickened in response to his touch. He cupped her breasts with his hands, massaging them gently and watching his actions in the mirror. There was something incredibly erotic about seeing their reflections in the mirror like this and feeling the weight of her in his hands, inhaling the subtle scent of her fragrant skin and feeling the rising heat that came from her body.

"Are you playing voyeur tonight?" she asked.

Her voice was husky, and when her eyes met his in the mirror, they shone with arousal.

"Do you like that?" he countered.

"Only if I get to watch, too," she replied, her voice catching on a hitch of breath.

Desire surged through him, making his fingers tremble as he touched her, clouding his mind to the point where he could barely think. Her hands closed over his, pressing them more firmly into her soft, malleable flesh and guiding him to gently squeeze her nipples. Her head fell back on his shoulder, her eyes glittering as she continued to watch their hands on her body. A flush spread across her chest and her cheeks. She guided one of his hands down over her belly to the apex of her thighs. He felt her shiver in response as his fingertip brushed against her clitoris.

"Again," she demanded.

Always a gentleman, he did his best to oblige. She let go of his hand and threaded her fingers up through his hair, her nails scraping his scalp as he circled the nub of nerve endings—occasionally touching it, pressing it, grazing it ever so slightly before letting his hand sweep away to dip into the core of her. She was wet, so wet, and he was equally as hard.

"Stand up," he directed. He helped her to her feet and pushed the stool away. "Good. Now put your hands on the dressing table."

"You're so bossy," she teased.

He ran his hand down her back to her buttocks and gave her a little slap. Her eyes flared in the mirror and she bit her bottom lip.

"And you're cheeky," he said with a smile as he loosened the tie on his pajamas and let them fall to his feet.

He stroked himself, letting her watch his reflection in the mirror.

"Oh no, that can't be what you plan to do," she said with a smile and swayed her hips sensuously. "Not when there are much better options available."

"I like being a man with options. What would you suggest?"

"You're a clever kind of guy. I think you've got this, don't you?"

He stroked one hand down her spine to the cleft of her buttocks and felt her body grow taut beneath his touch. He stroked the lush globes of her bottom, then delved lower, deeper, to where the heat and moisture of her body awaited his possession.

"This, you mean?"

He slid one finger inside her and stroked her deeply—feeling her body clench against him.

Her voice shook when she spoke. "Something like that, yes. But I think you can do better."

"She wants better?" he murmured. "Then her wish is my command."

He positioned himself behind her and guided the swollen head of his penis to her, pressing himself gently until he was only just inside the entrance to her body. He forced himself to hold back, his hands now resting on the curves of her hips. Her inner muscles tightened around him, driving a groan from him and sending a bolt of pleasure rocketing from his tip through his entire body.

"Galen, please. Don't tease me, not about this, not anymore. I want you deep inside me. I need you."

It was those last three words that proved his undoing. He threw restraint to the wind and allowed his body to surge within hers. Peyton's hands tightened into fists on the dressing table as he filled her. A gasp of pleasure escaped her. She pressed against him and the sensation of her buttocks against his groin made him move again, and again, until all he could think about was the pleasure filling his body, filling hers. On the brink of letting go, he paused and reached for her, his fingers deftly finding her pleasure spot and massaging her right there. It took the lightest touch to set her off and he felt every paroxysm of pleasure as it swelled through her body and he gave himself up to his own release.

They were both shaking when he finally withdrew

from her moments later. She rose and turned to face
him, her arms sliding around his waist. The skin-to-
skin contact, their racing hearts and the perspira-
tion of their bodies gleaming in the light of the room
seemed like the perfect denouement to their joining.

"C'mon," he whispered against her hair. "Let's go
to bed."

Shortly afterward they were cuddled up in bed together, her head resting in the curve of his shoulder
and his arm around her body, his hand absently strok-
ing her silky skin. Galen flipped the master switch
that plunged the room into darkness and was beginning to slide into sleep when she spoke.

"Galen?"

"Mmm-hmm?"

"I think you should brush my hair more often."

He smiled and pulled her even tighter to him, his
heart filling with the words he suddenly wished he
could say. He loved her. The realization hit him with
a solid thump to his solar plexus as he turned the
thought around and around in his head. He loved her.
But did that mean anything if she didn't love him in
return?

She couldn't concentrate because her treacherous
mind kept spinning back to the way Galen had made
love to her last night. And it had been lovemaking,
not just sex. There'd been something about the way
he'd touched her, the way he'd lavished attention on
her, that had been more than what they'd done together before. The knowledge both thrilled and ter-

rified her. She'd barely dared consider that she could let another person get this close to her. She could feel herself wanting to let him inside every part of her, not just her body but her mind, as well, so they could truly be one together. But she couldn't let that happen. It wasn't what she'd set herself up to do and she'd learned a long time ago that deviation from her chosen path only led to heartbreak and disappointment.

Peyton saved her document again and stared blindly at the computer screen. This feature was no less aggressive than anything else she'd done. Oh sure, as Alice had so adroitly pointed out yesterday, it wasn't about anything as topical as an environmental or political issue, nor did it tread along the battlefields of far-flung places. But it did reflect the battlefield of her childhood, and the woman who'd single-handedly ensured that Peyton's life would never be the same again from the moment she'd fired her dad.

She thought for a moment of the bitter man he still was today. Of the blame and anger that had become his constant refrain, which had, in turn, pushed away anyone who'd tried to love or care for him, including Peyton. How different her life would have been had Alice Horvath not destroyed the very fabric of her family. Peyton sighed and rested her hands back on the keyboard. She had to somehow remove personal bias from this profile of the Horvath matriarch. Let the facts speak for themselves.

She printed out the document and rose from her chair, pacing her office as the papers began to stack up in the printer tray. Once the article was printed, she grabbed one of her favorite red pens for editing and the bunch of papers and went downstairs onto the deck.

She hadn't been editing for long when she felt her cell phone vibrate in her pocket. A quick glance at the screen confirmed it was Ellie's school. She put down her pen and answered the call.

"Ms. Earnshaw, I'm sorry to bother you. I did try to get hold of Mr. Horvath but he's apparently in a meeting."

"Not a problem. Is it Ellie? Is something wrong?"

"She appears to have an upset stomach. We feel it best if she went home for the rest of today."

"No problem. I'll be right there."

Peyton disconnected the call, shoved her phone in her jeans pocket and reached for the stack of papers she had on the table in front of her. Just then, a massive gust of wind caught the papers and ruffled them across the table and the deck. Peyton frantically picked them up, counting them to ensure she had them all. Yes, every last one accounted for. She closed the glass sliding door behind her as she raced to the breakfast room, where she'd left her bag and car keys yesterday, and shoved the papers in her bag before shooting through to the garage, getting her car out and heading toward the school.

Ellie was very definitely the worse for wear when she got there, tearful and pale with a sickly cast to her skin that made Peyton glad she always carried a spare towel or two in her car.

"C'mon, sweetheart, let's get home and into bed,"

she said, putting an arm around Ellie and picking up her schoolbag.

Ellie fell asleep in the car on the way home, a sign she definitely wasn't feeling well because she was usually full of energy and chatter right up until bedtime. Peyton felt her heart tug in sympathy for the child. As she drove down the driveway to the house, she saw Galen's car up ahead outside the garage. She hadn't expected him home this early and thanked her lucky stars she hadn't left the unproofed article lying anywhere.

She parked, hooked her bag over her arm and went around the car to open Ellie's door. The poor kid was still out cold and Peyton didn't want to wake her. There was nothing else to do but to carry her inside. She unhooked Ellie's seat belt and lifted the little girl into her arms. She was heavier than she looked, Peyton realized as she made her way to the door.

To her relief, the door swung open the moment she approached.

"I got a message from the school," Galen said, stepping forward. "I called back, but they said you'd just left with her, so I came here instead to wait for you both. Is she okay?"

"Probably just a tummy bug," Peyton said. "She doesn't seem to have a fever."

"Can I take her for you?"

"I think I can manage, but maybe you could take my bag before I drop it?"

The minute the words were out of her mouth she regretted the suggestion. She hadn't zipped her tote shut in her hurry and her article was jammed right there at the top, in full view of anyone.

"Just leave it here in the foyer. I'll grab it later," she said quickly as Galen reached to slide it off the crook of her elbow.

At that moment Ellie stirred in her arms and groaned. "I'm going to be sick!"

Peyton rushed toward the guest bathroom, thankfully only a few steps away. Galen dropped her bag to the floor and followed in hot pursuit.

So this was parenting, Peyton thought as she brushed her hand over the exhausted little girl's forehead after they'd changed her into pajamas and settled her in her bedroom.

"Will you stay with me?" Ellie asked weakly.

"Sure."

Galen hovered at the end of Ellie's bed, watching the little girl with a worried expression on his face. "Would you like me to stay, too?"

"I want Peyton," Ellie grumbled listlessly.

"I'm right here," Peyton said. "I'll sit with you until you fall asleep, okay?"

Ellie nodded. Galen moved away from the bed.

"It seems I'm not needed," he murmured.

"For now."

"You'll be okay?"

Peyton looked at Ellie, whose eyes were already drooping closed. "Yeah, we'll be fine. I'll just stay with her a while until she's fast asleep again."

Galen put a hand on her shoulder and she instantly felt the warmth of his fingers through her thin shirt.

"You're good with her, y'know?"

"Thanks," she managed through a throat that was a little choked up. She'd never had the chance to soothe her own baby's tears or illnesses.

As Galen left the room, Peyton turned her gaze back to the little girl in the bed. She looked so very small right now, so helpless. Peyton was swamped with emotion. Was this what parenthood was like? This overwhelming fear that something could go wrong at any time and snatch your precious child away combined with a love that constantly grew and evolved as the child did? She'd given away her chance at experiencing all of this and hadn't allowed herself to ever grow close enough to another person to risk having to face doing such a thing again.

Peyton reached out a hand to gently brush Ellie's brow, telling herself she was just checking for fever. She didn't want to love this little girl and yet the thought of leaving had begun to fill her with dread.

But she couldn't turn back. She'd set her path. The words Alice had spoken the other day came back to ring in her ears—*be careful where you tread*—and sent a shiver down her spine.

Sixteen

Galen changed out of his suit, took a quick shower and put on jeans and a T-shirt before heading downstairs again. He felt conflicted. For several months it had just been him and the kiddo, and he'd liked that. But, he reminded himself, getting married was something he'd chosen to do so that Ellie would always have someone to fall back on in those times when he couldn't be there. Times like today.

When he got downstairs he saw Peyton's bag where he'd dropped it. He'd teased her about being Mary Poppins the first time he'd seen the size of the thing. Smiling at the memory, he went over to pick it up but, as he did so, a sheaf of papers spilled from inside onto the tiled floor. He gathered the papers up and was about to shove them back in her bag when a name caught his eye. Alice Horvath.

Was this the article she was so busy working on lately? Peyton had refused to discuss it with him and he knew, out of respect for her, he should put the papers back in her bag and forget about them. But the mention of his grandmother had piqued his interest. Galen went into the sitting room, sat down on a couch, telling himself he was just going to skim but the content forced him to read them in earnest. His temper rose as he realized that the article was very specifically about his grandmother and it wasn't flattering. Galen put the papers very carefully back in Peyton's bag and fought the urge to thunder up the stairs and demand she explain what the hell she was up to.

He got up and went outside. Staring into the distance, he wondered what had driven Peyton to write such a piece. He knew his grandmother had to have made some enemies along the way; a person didn't carve out the success she had without making a few. But this article had taken a very dark look at Nagy's business practices, even drawing into question her methods for matchmaking with Match Made in Marriage.

The sense of betrayal he felt ballooned as he considered how Peyton had been welcomed with open arms into the family. It was all the worse for the fact that he now knew he'd fallen in love with her, prickly nature and all. There had to be a very specific motivation behind Peyton's actions and he needed to work out what that was and stop her from sending this piece out. Given Nagy's heart surgery and her age, he was prepared to do anything to protect her and knew the rest of the family would close ranks around her, too. But he couldn't alert any of them to this yet—if he did, they'd shun Peyton immediately. And if he could turn Peyton around to see the Nagy he, his family and most of her employees loved devotedly, then there'd be no damage done. First, however, he needed to understand why she'd done this.

He had no idea how long he had to investigate his wife, but he knew he had to act swiftly. Galen went into the office he kept downstairs, fired up his laptop and did a basic search on Peyton. Very little came up under her maiden name aside from her publishing accolades. It made him suspicious that there was no mention of her prior to her career as a journalist. Normally, there was something, somewhere, about people. A sporting achievement, an award given while at college. But it was as if she'd popped into the world fully formed and hard at work from the age of about twenty-one. Which probably meant she had legally changed her name at some point.

There was one person who likely had the information he sought. The very person he was trying to protect in all this—Alice. But how on earth would he get it out of her? She guarded the information surrounding the people involved in her matches zealously— and would continue to do so even knowing she was under attack. He shook his head. Somehow, he had to find a way that didn't involve his grandmother.

It took several days before the investigator he'd engaged got back to him. What he read was disturbing. It seemed that on graduating college, Peyton had assumed her mother's maiden name. He could understand why. From what the investigator had uncovered, Peyton's family life, if it could be called that, had been grossly dysfunctional. He could understand why anyone would want to turn their back on that. But even though she'd changed her name, and for all intents and purposes appeared to have little to no contact with her father, she still supported the man financially. As if she was trying to make up for something when, as far as Galen could see, she had nothing to make up for. In fact, she'd been very much the victim.

And no wonder she'd had such empathy for Ellie. She'd been a similar age when her mom had been diagnosed with multiple sclerosis and her mother's downturn in health had been unexpectedly rapid, exacerbated, no doubt, by the fact they had no medical insurance once Peyton's dad had been fired from Horvath Corporation. That little snippet had come as a surprise.

Learning that Peyton's father had been the chief financial officer at Horvath Corporation but had been let go on suspicion of embezzlement had shocked him. The evidence against the man had been damning; in fact, Alice would have had every right to have pressed criminal charges against him. But given the man's situation at home, Galen had no doubt his grandmother had chosen the high road. Getting rid of Magnus Maitland had been her only choice.

The PI had done a little background search on Maitland, discovering that he'd held a raft of short-term positions over the years since his dismissal. Not one of

them had approached the salary he'd earned at Horvath
Corporation, which must have been galling to a man
with his qualifications, let alone worrying financially.
It seemed that his wife's illness had eaten up every
penny of savings they'd had, but there was strong evidence that they'd lived well outside their means while
he was at Horvath Corporation, which had only made
matters worse for them when he was fired.

Galen shook his head. Poor Peyton. She hadn't
stood a chance with her father's white-collar crime,
her mother's illness, being torn away from the home
she'd grown up in and moving out of state. And then,
to cap it off, to have had a brief and obviously intense relationship with a young man on the brink of
deployment and to find herself pregnant and alone
after his death. Was it any wonder she'd developed a
hard shell of distrust and caution?

But to have written this article the way she had?
That spoke to a level of planning years in the making. And had she somehow manipulated their marriage match? The idea was outrageous and yet made
perfect sense. Was it possible that his grandmother
had been tricked by someone with access to the Match
Made in Marriage systems? Had Peyton married him
purely to get better access to information about his
grandmother?

And after she released her article to the world,
what then? Did she plan to simply up and leave him
and Ellie? Did she not care for either of them one bit?

He thought about the woman who'd spent the night
sleeping in a chair beside Ellie's bed after the tummy

bug incident. That didn't match up with the woman who'd written the vile piece of journalism he'd read the other day. But the woman who'd written that article was well capable of doing the things he suspected. Of manipulating and using others to her advantage. And right now Galen was feeling very used.

There was only one thing for it. He had to confront her.

Galen had been distant these past few days and Peyton couldn't help feeling she was responsible for that, somehow. Even tonight, his office door remained firmly shut, and when Ellie went to tell him their dinner was ready, he'd asked her to tell Peyton to leave his plate covered and he'd get to it later. It was only after Ellie had retired for the night that she dared knock on his door and beard the lion in his den, so to speak.

"What?" he said, looking up.

He'd been running his hands through his hair, which stuck out every which way in complete contrast to the smooth executive who'd left the house this morning. Peyton gave him a smile.

"Is everything okay? You sound distracted."

"No, everything is not okay. Take a seat. We need to talk."

She felt a knot form in her stomach. He'd never spoken to her in that tone before. From day one, Galen had been lighthearted, teasingly coercive or passionate. Never this serious. She settled on the small sofa tucked against the wall and waited for him to speak.

He rubbed at his eyes a moment and then drilled her with a look that made her feel like an insect on a pin.

"I'd like you to tell me about your article."

"I told you before," she hedged. "It's about strong women in business."

"Peyton, we both know that isn't true."

"Have you been sneaking into my computer?"

"No, I haven't. But I will admit I have read your article about Nagy." He briefly outlined what had happened the afternoon Ellie had come home sick.

"You had no right to read that," Peyton said firmly.

"You had no right to write lies about my grandmother."

"Everything I've said in that article is true."

"Really? Are your sources legitimate? I notice you don't refer to anyone by their real name. Not even your own father."

"Alice fired my father without adequate proof and without an independent investigation. Have you got any idea of what that did to my family?"

"So this is about revenge, then." His voice was cold and his face set like stone.

"You had better believe it. Not everyone has the chance to see the world through rose-tinted glasses like you Horvaths do. You don't even see the truth in one another. When your grandmother fired my father, she as good as murdered my mom. Without Dad's benefits we couldn't afford to stay near her doctors, let alone afford her ongoing care when she started to suffer from seizures. What Alice did to us was unspeakable. The shame of what she'd accused my dad of was bad enough for Mom without having to sell our home and move away from everyone we knew. But your grandmother couldn't resist going one step further, could she? She had to go and smear my father's name so it became impossible for him to find a decent job.

"Do you know what it did to him to have to take on work detailing cars and cleaning bathrooms in office buildings just so we could eat? It crushed him that he couldn't provide for Mom's health care. It wasn't her MS that killed her. It was a broken spirit. Broken by your grandmother."

"Your father made his choices."

"Oh, of course you'd say that," Peyton spit in disgust. "All of you are the same. I had begun to think you were different. That maybe I was making a mistake. The article you saw, that was a draft. I'd even begun to wonder if I was doing the right thing. But your attitude right now is typical of what I'd always believed your family to be. You're so damned self-righteous. You don't believe for a second you could be in the wrong. You've never had to struggle and fight for anything. You have no idea what it's like for the rest of us, and you never will. Yes, your grandparents built a dynasty. But they did it at the cost of other people's happiness, and it's past time people got to see the real Alice Horvath. She's not the warm, friendly character you all portray. She has a backbone of steel and ice water runs in her veins. She had no compassion for my family, none, and that killed my mother! My father struggled to raise me and, because of your grandmother, I couldn't raise my own daughter."

Galen stiffened under her verbal assault. His face, already stern, now looked as though it had been carved from granite, and his blue eyes turned glacial. In this moment he looked more like his grandmother than Peyton had ever seen him, and it shocked her.

"I think you had better stop there," he said very carefully. "Before you say anything more you might regret."

"I regret nothing," she answered, determined not to give an inch.

"Really? And what is this all for? You already told me you and your father barely speak."

"We never got the chance to have a normal father-daughter relationship thanks to Alice!"

"Did you really think that writing this muck about my grandmother would turn back the clock for him and you? That you'd be able to rebuild the relationship you think you should have had with him?"

Peyton couldn't speak for the pain that had built like a giant burr behind her breastbone.

"Tell me, Peyton, what did you hope to gain from our marriage?" Galen continued. "Material for that article? Was that all?"

She nodded and pursed her lips. She didn't trust herself to speak right now, not when she could hear the note of hurt beneath the anger in his voice. She'd told herself from the start that the end justified the means. Her parents deserved to have their truth be told, both them and the others who'd been unfairly dismissed from Horvath Corporation. She was their crusader, their voice in the darkness, their right from wrong. She wasn't about to let some stupid emotions get in the way of all of that.

"So the whole thing is a sham for you—is that what you're saying?"

"Don't put words in my mouth."

She thought it wouldn't matter—that she'd be able to keep her feelings secure behind the rock-solid walls she'd erected around her for all her adult life—but faced with his anger, his disappointment, his hurt, she knew those walls would never be high or deep enough to save her from the pain that had begun to unravel inside. By attacking Alice Horvath, she'd hurt Galen deeply, and by hurting him, she'd hurt herself.

"Oh, I think we've probably both said enough for today, don't you?" His voice vibrated with pain and fury. "I want you out of here, out of my life and away from Ellie before you can poison her, too."

His words stung her like the lash of a whip. Logically she knew he had every right to demand she leave this house immediately, but the reality of it was excruciating.

"I'll pack and leave in the morning after Ellie's gone to school."

"Thank you." He bit the words out as if they left a bad taste in his mouth. "I'll sleep in one of the other rooms tonight."

"No, don't. I'll go back to my room."

He acknowledged her offer with a lift of his head. Silence stretched between them interminably. Peyton felt as though she should say something but she was frozen in place, still filled with shock that he'd discovered what she was doing before she could extricate herself from what had become a messy situation. She snapped herself out of it, spun on her heel and left Galen's office to go upstairs.

In her old room she sat on the bed. She'd never imagined he'd find out. Somehow she'd always thought she could just do her thing, release her article and walk away. But it turned out nothing was simple anymore. People complicated things. Which was one of the reasons she'd never allowed anyone to get close to her since her baby's father had died, she reminded herself.

But Galen had looked stricken. Not just because of what she'd said in her article, but on another level. As if he'd begun to develop feelings for her that went deeper than being bed buddies and coparenting Ellie. She felt the sharp pain behind her breastbone again.

Peyton tried to do what she'd always done: default to anger. Anger was a useful emotion—not like love or sorrow or any of the weaknesses that left you exposed to other people. Anger was something you could work with. She sat where she was and allowed it to grow, stoking it with the list of Alice's transgressions, which had broken her family into tiny splintered pieces.

The list was long—from her mom's inability to pay for treatment to the dog they'd had to give away. From her father's bitter emotional distance to Peyton's desperation to find love with a stranger. From finding out she was pregnant by a man she barely knew, but believed she'd loved, to learning of his death and having to give up custody of her newborn daughter. Oh yes, and then there was all the financial hardship in between. Being that child at school wearing clothing from the thrift store, clothing that one of the popular kids' moms had left there, and being ridiculed for it. All of it could be laid squarely at Alice Horvath's feet.

So, Galen wanted her gone from here. Her hands curled into fists at her sides. She couldn't wait to leave.

And Ellie? Would leaving Ellie behind be easy? No, of course not. But she'd said goodbye to her own baby—a child she'd nurtured and carried for forty weeks and three days before giving birth. A child she'd left in the nursery as she'd walked out of the hospital and turned her back on motherhood forever. This idyll with Ellie had been a taste of what she might have had—but she couldn't afford to dwell on that. Instead, she had to let the black hole that had opened deep inside her consume the love she'd developed for the little girl.

And what about Galen? No, she couldn't think about him. Couldn't give words to how she felt about him—how he'd made her feel. She'd known from the start that getting married would be a risk. That was what her work was about. Taking that risk. Pushing that envelope. But it came at a very high cost.

Seventeen

Peyton stripped the bed in her room and balled the sheets up in her arms. She'd barely slept a wink during the night and at about 4:00 a.m. she'd given up entirely and begun to pack her things. She hadn't brought much—knowing in the back of her mind that this wouldn't last forever.

And now it was over. She felt as if she'd suffered a bereavement. There was no triumph in the piece she'd written. No sense of completion. Just this yawning, aching hole deep inside her, knowing that today she was walking away from Galen and Ellie forever. She'd spent a lot of last night thinking about Galen's reaction, about his anger. Not to mention his protectiveness toward Ellie.

She'd known the article would affect everyone associated with Alice in one way or another. Even Ellie viewed Alice as a much-loved great-grandmother. The knowledge that the fallout would hurt the little girl pricked like needles under Peyton's skin. Hurting Ellie had never been on her agenda. She'd just wanted the world to see Alice for who she really was. And yes, as Galen had suggested yesterday, maybe rebuild a better relationship with her father.

A knock at her bedroom door startled her. "Yes?"

"It's me. Can I come in?" Galen's voice sounded strained.

"Of course," she said.

Her body clenched on a wash of pure physical reaction as he came into her room and shut the door behind him. Dressed in a dark navy suit and pale blue business shirt and tie, he was the epitome of a Horvath—power and success exuded from every pore. He looked tired, with shadows beneath his eyes, and she felt a spiteful tinge of satisfaction that he'd probably had no more rest last night than she had.

"Look, about our discussion last night."

"I think you made your wishes perfectly clear. I'll leave as soon as Ellie's safely at school."

"Yes, well, there's been a change in plans. I've been called to go to Japan for urgent meetings. I had hoped that perhaps Maggie could live in while I was away so Ellie's timetable wouldn't be disrupted, but she is unable to do so. Can I ask you to please stay on, at least until my return?"

"Well, make up your mind, won't you?" Peyton

couldn't help the irritated tone in her voice. "First you want me out of here, now you want me to stay?"

"This isn't my preference, Peyton. You're the one who made a mockery of our marriage, our family."

Oh, he knew how to hurt her and, she reluctantly admitted, she deserved it.

"Fine. I could do with the time to make some arrangements anyway. How long will you be gone?"

"A week, possibly ten days." He shifted, looking uncomfortable. "If I could have had anyone else here, I would. But Ellie is bonded to you and without me here…" His voice trailed off.

"I'll stay."

"Thank you." He turned to leave but then turned around and faced her again. "And you will say nothing to Ellie about us separating. I will deal with that myself on my return. Understood?"

"Understood."

Her throat closed up. She could barely breathe, let alone speak. While his face remained as implacable as it had been last night, in his gaze she could see the turmoil and hurt. Turmoil and hurt she'd caused. He closed his eyes briefly and when he reopened them all those feelings had been wiped away and replaced with a resolve that reminded her very much of his grandmother.

"I'll call Ellie before bed every night."

She nodded and watched as he opened the door and left. She waited until she heard the front door slam before she managed to pull herself together and head downstairs. Ellie was perched at the breakfast table, finishing her cereal. Maggie was humming happily in the kitchen. It was like any other morning, except it wasn't.

Galen was exhausted. The return flight from Tokyo had been full of turbulence, and while that didn't normally bother him, Ellie's fears related to losing her parents had weighed on his mind and made him anxious to get home.

His driver dropped him at the front door of the house and he grabbed his case and let himself inside. The house was quiet, so quiet that he wondered whether or not Peyton had already moved out. He shook his head. She might be a devious piece of work but she'd never abandon Ellie. He was sure of that.

He heard a sound on the staircase. Peyton.

The sight of her was like a punch to the gut. Every cell in his body went into overdrive. He'd missed their physical connection with an ache that had been present the entire time he'd been away. Ten long days and even longer nights. But, he reminded himself, he'd better get used to it. She was out of here very soon. In fact, now that he was back, it may as well be today.

"All packed?" he asked, dispensing with any of the usual greetings.

"Not quite," she answered.

He could see his words had irritated her. Good, because he was irritated, too. Why did this all have to be such a debacle? He'd talked to his grandmother while he was away, probing for information about Peyton without telling Nagy exactly why he couldn't just ask his wife directly. Nagy had been tight-lipped, advising him to stop beating around the bush and to speak to Peyton. But how did he tell Nagy that Peyton would be out of all their lives very soon, and that they'd need to collectively batten down the hatches as a family if the fallout from Peyton's damned article was as bad as he suspected it might be?

Galen dragged his thoughts back to the woman in front of him.

"I'm back. You don't need to be here anymore," he said bluntly.

"Your grandmother is coming to visit. Tomorrow. Would you like me gone before or after she arrives?"

Galen bit back the frustrated retort on the edge of his tongue. "My preference doesn't matter. She will obviously expect to see us both. You'd better stay until we find out what she wants."

"Fine."

He watched Peyton stalk away and heard a door upstairs slam soon after. Then he dropped into the nearest chair. What a damn mess—and what the hell was Nagy up to, making a spur-of-the-moment visit like this?

Peyton heard the car pull up in the driveway and straightened herself before going to open the front door. Maggie had been instructed to make up the downstairs guest suite in preparation for Alice's arrival and had even agreed to extra hours to ensure that every whim that Alice might express could be met. Ellie had been over the moon with excitement when she'd heard the old lady was coming to stay. Peyton certainly didn't feel the same. And there Alice was, standing in the doorway, looking a little older, a little frailer than she had a few weeks ago, when Peyton had interviewed her.

"Alice, welcome. Please, come inside," Peyton said stiffly.

"Are you the sole member of the welcoming committee?" the older woman asked, offering her cheek for a kiss.

Peyton bent and brushed her lips against the wrinkled skin, and was surprised to feel the press of Alice's lips against her cheek.

"It's good to see you, my dear. How have you been? Working too hard, by the look of you."

"I could say the same about you," Peyton responded in kind and was rewarded with a chuckle of approval.

"I like you, Peyton. I wasn't sure I would, but I really do."

Peyton took a step back—Alice's words were both a surprise and a shock. Well, she might like her now, but that was sure to change.

"Now, where are my grandson and my great-granddaughter?"

"Ellie will be home from school shortly and Galen is on his way here as we speak. An unexpected call held him up."

He'd texted her earlier, saying he'd been delayed. Texting seemed to be the only way they were able to remain civil to one another these days.

"Will Ellie be joining us at dinner tonight?" Alice asked, giving Peyton a sharp look.

"No, it's a school night. We thought it best if she not stay out too late."

Alice nodded. "Hmm, probably just as well."

"Just as well?"

"We have a lot to discuss. Now, if you don't mind, I think I'll take a little beauty rest. You could do with following my example."

Peyton blinked in surprise at the insult. Then she realized Alice was teasing. She didn't quite know how she felt about that but opted for a smile. "Have a good rest, Alice. The bed in the guest room is all made up. I'll make sure Ellie doesn't disturb you."

She rolled Alice's suitcase into the bedroom and hoisted it onto a stand for her, then left the old woman to her devices. Probably casting spells and mixing up potions, she thought with an uncharitable smirk. But then she stopped herself. Alice had said she liked her, and the woman was known to be painfully blunt about things. The knowledge that she'd somehow broken past the barrier of acceptance was bittersweet and filled her with unaccustomed warmth. That was rapidly quenched with the icy reality of how this family would treat her once her article went out. She'd delayed sending it to her editor, telling herself she needed to triple fact-check every word. But she knew that everything was perfect and ready to go. All she had to do was push Send. Yet, somehow, something held her back.

Was it the fear of how it would affect Ellie? she

asked herself as she settled on one of the loungers on the deck. Or was it the fact that when it went to publication, she'd be closing the door on any chance of ever mending fences with Galen? She'd never felt a single qualm about any word she'd written before. Why was this different?

She felt that all-too-familiar tug at her heart when she considered what it would be like when she walked out that front door and never came back. Never saw Galen or Ellie again. Grief swelled inside her, threatening to reduce her to tears. But she wasn't a crier, she told herself. She was strong. She'd made the tough decisions and survived before and she would again. But this time it was different. This time she'd be walking away from the man she loved.

Peyton closed her eyes and allowed herself to finally admit that she was in love with Galen. She'd never expected to fall for him, never wanted to. But now that she'd admitted it to herself, she found she couldn't neatly box up her feelings and hide them away like she'd always done in the past. She loved him and she knew this article was hurting him, and yet she still owed it to her mom and dad to put it out there.

You could cut the air between Galen and Peyton with a knife, Alice observed as they were seated at a waterfront table at one of her favorite restaurants in Port Ludlow. Time was not making this match any easier. Alice sighed inwardly. This wasn't how she imagined things progressing at all. These two would regret this for the rest of their lives if she didn't step up and fix things. She only hoped she wasn't too late.

After they'd placed their orders, Alice settled herself more comfortably in her chair and stared at the two of them.

"Which one of you is going to tell me what's up between you?"

Silence, although her question did make them look at one another.

"Peyton, how about you start?" she coaxed.

She knew the girl was unlikely to sugarcoat anything.

"We've decided to separate. Things are not working out."

"Really?" Alice frowned. "Is that all you have to say on the matter?"

Peyton started fiddling with her napkin, then her water glass, then placed her hands in her lap and looked straight across the table at Alice. "Really. I need to be honest with you. Galen discovered that I lied about my motives for entering our marriage."

"Is that so?" Alice raised a brow and looked at her grandson. "Galen?"

He nodded, clearly not trusting himself to speak.

"So your motive to marry my grandson to be able to get dirt on me has upset him?" Alice stated calmly and reached for a breadstick. She snapped the end off and popped it in her mouth, chewing thoughtfully as she took in Galen's and Peyton's identical, somewhat comical, looks of disbelief.

"You knew?" Peyton blurted.

"Of course I knew. But the facts are the facts. You and Galen are the most compatible match for one another. Once you get this bee out of your bonnet, I think you two will be very happy together."

"You can't expect us to remain married after this," Galen spluttered. "She has manipulated us and outright lied. I certainly can't trust her and I don't want her around Ellie, either."

"Ah, yes. Ellie." Alice looked down at her plate, searching for the right words. This was such a sensitive situation. Had she overreached herself?

"What about Ellie?" Peyton sounded truly concerned and had paled considerably.

"Have a sip of water, dear. I don't want you fainting on us," Alice said. "The situation with Ellie is complicated. Peyton, I've followed your life carefully since your childhood. I know it wasn't easy for you and you struggled at times, but when I discovered you were alone and pregnant, I knew I had to step in and offer help."

"You what? You've spied on me since childhood? You arranged the private adoption? What is this? Some kind of *Twilight Zone* episode?"

Peyton was incredulous and Galen equally dumbstruck.

"It does make me sound like a meddling old woman but I knew your parents well. I owed it to your mother to keep an eye on you. You see, your father not only betrayed our company, he betrayed a friendship, as well."

"You were no friend of my mother. You left her to die."

"And I will regret that for the rest of my days. Your father cut off all contact between us when you moved to Oregon." Alice blinked hard and fought to compose herself. "Now, regarding the adoption—Nick and Sarah had been in our employ for quite a while and they befriended Galen and made his transition from upstart college graduate to astute and compassionate CEO a much easier one than if he'd had to work with anyone else. I knew of their struggles to have a child. I knew of your predicament. It seemed to me to be the best solution at the time, and it cleared your student loans and medical bills, did it not? Made the path easier for you to truly get ahead in your career? A career you have done exceptionally well in, too, I might add. And while I'm on the subject, how is your latest work coming along?"

Peyton just stared at her, dumbstruck. Galen was not so stricken.

"Her latest work is a pack of filthy lies!" he interjected.

"It is not! Can't you even hear your grandmother now? She's been pulling strings and meddling in everyone's lives for years! Mine included." Peyton slapped her hand on the table. "I can't do this. I can't sit here and pretend to be civil and enjoy dinner."

She stood up and started to walk away. Alice reached out and caught her hand.

"Sit down, my dear, please. I have something to say to you and you *will* do me the courtesy of listening. After that, stay if you want to, or leave. The choice is entirely yours."

To Alice's relief, Peyton sat down again. All eyes in the restaurant were turned to them. Alice gave the other diners a quelling glance and all turned back to their meals immediately. In the meantime a waiter hurried over with their plates and another poured their wine. Alice lifted her glass and tipped it to the others.

"To your good health," she said.

Galen and Peyton automatically followed her lead but she noted that Galen didn't sip his wine, instead placing the glass back on the table with careful deliberation. Her poor boy. He was in turmoil. She could see it as plain as the nose on his face. He'd fallen in love with Peyton, too; she could see that. It was why he was hurting so badly now. A pang of regret flicked along a nerve in her back and she flinched before taking a steadying breath and preparing to make her statement to Peyton. Maybe after this Galen would be free to admit his love and to fight for his woman. She could only hope.

"Now, Peyton, I imagine that you have written what you believe to be the truth."

"I know it's the truth. I've done my research. I've checked my sources," she said stubbornly.

"The thing is, there are always many sides to a story. If you aren't careful, my dear, you will end up repeating your father's mistakes and, like him, end up irrevocably hurting the ones you love most."

Peyton's nostrils flared as she drew in a sharp breath. "You are the one who hurt our family."

"My dear, I suggest you need to rely a little less on personal memories and go straight to the source of all your discontent. I tried to protect you and your mother then, and once you've checked your research more carefully, you will find that you've allowed your father's somewhat skewed version of the events of that time to overcome your usual reason and ability to report rationally. I know you're at the top of your profession, Peyton, but I fear you are well off the mark with your current assignment.

"Can I also say that I found your approaching and exploiting your old college friend Michelle beneath the caliber of reporter I have always thought you to be."

"You haven't fired her, too, have you? It wasn't her fault," Peyton interjected.

"No, of course it wasn't. Michelle came to me right away and told me exactly what was going on. I allowed her to give you access to specific information because you deserved at least that. But twisting that information to suit your own needs, that is not what I expected of you. I know you think you circumvented the matchmaking process with Galen, but I can assure you that you did not. Michelle had no control over the outcome of who Galen was to marry that day. You and he are the perfect match for one another. It is my goal to see my grandson and my new great-granddaughter happy. You also deserve to be happy, Peyton. But your happiness, and now that of Galen and Ellie, is entirely up to you and what you decide to do next."

Eighteen

Peyton parked her car on the bluff of the windswept beach and got out to scan the sand that stretched out below. This was a lonely and godforsaken stretch of the Oregon coast. It suited her father perfectly. In the distance, she could make him out, a large surf rod embedded in the sand next to him. He stood there, oblivious, the wind buffeting him, a light rain soaking him. Self-contained in all his animosity and resentment at the injustices of the world. She swallowed hard. This wasn't going to be easy. The last time she'd seen him, after she'd given Ellie up for adoption, he'd basically told her not to bother visiting again.

His words had been calculated to hurt and do as much damage as possible. But here she was, nearly ten years later, gearing up for another onslaught of his vitriol and unhappiness, all in the pursuit of truth. Would he even give her that much? she wondered. Or would he just retreat back to his basic cabin off the beach and continue to wallow in his misery?

She never understood how a man who'd appeared to have it all when she was a child could have come this low. But now that she was older and, she hoped, wiser, she could begin to understand.

Peyton locked her rental car and started down the weathered steps that led to the beach. The wind whipped around her, throwing sand at her skin with stinging intensity, while waves crashed loudly on the beach beside her. He must have seen her approach, but he didn't react until she was almost upon him.

"You're back."

He didn't sound happy about it.

"Yes, I'm back, Dad. How are you doing?"

He shrugged. "What do you want?"

"Some answers."

"Have you done that article yet?"

Peyton sighed. The last time she'd tried to talk to her father he'd been about to hang up on her, until she'd told him what she was planning to do. "Not yet, no."

"What's taking you so long? I told you what that bitch did to me. About time she got a taste of her own medicine."

Peyton shoved her hands in the pockets of her jacket and stared out at the waves and their inexorable assault on the sandy beach. She weighed the questions she'd been practicing in the back of her mind on the long drive here. It was time to ask them, even if it may well end up being the last time her father ever spoke to her. She turned to face him.

"Dad?"

"What?"

His response was abrupt. Hardly an invitation to open up for a deep and meaningful conversation, but she had to press on. She deserved to know the truth.

"What really happened when you lost your job at Horvath Corporation? Did you steal from them?"

Her father stared out at the sea and the lines on his face appeared to deepen beneath her gaze. His lips firmed, then trembled as they parted on a huff of breath. He seemed to grow physically smaller in stature, his shoulders more bowed, his head more bent. His hands curled into fists at his sides.

"It was only meant to be a loan," he said so softly she barely heard him speak.

"A loan?" she prompted when he fell silent again.

"Your mother deserved the best of everything. It's what she grew up with and I'd promised her that if she chose me, her life didn't have to change. I was overstretched financially, but once I was on the treadmill, I just couldn't get off it. It gave me a buzz to give your mom the latest gadget, the best garden, the latest model car, everything. At first I only borrowed a little bit to tide us over from paycheck to paycheck. I'd reimburse it and no one was any the wiser. But then your mom got sick and I got behind in returning the money, and eventually I had to borrow greater and greater sums. It became harder to hide it and I had to adjust some of the financial reports to ensure that no one would pick up the discrepancies."

"Why didn't you just tell Mom we were living beyond our means? Why didn't we downsize sooner, before you needed to take money from the company?"

He laughed but it was a bitter and twisted sound. "And lose your mother's love? I couldn't bear to see the disappointment on her face if I told her I wasn't what I pretended to be. It was my role to provide for you both. She was the love of my life, my whole reason for being on this earth. I had to be able to offer her the moon and the stars and more. She came from a wealthy family, she had everything, but she chose me. I had to show her I was as good as the people who'd cut her off when she married me. The people who, even when she became ill, would have nothing to do with her. No help, not a letter, not a phone call, nothing. I had to be everything to her. I wanted to be everything to her. And I turned out to be nothing, after all."

A solitary tear worked its way down his weathered cheek and Peyton felt her heart twist in compassion to see her proud, if misguided, father let down his guard this way. What he'd done had been incredibly wrong, but he had done it for love. Peyton had grown up believing her mom's parents had died, but this revelation from her father made her realize that she had a whole other family out there. More people who didn't want her. But she couldn't afford to dwell on that now.

"Dad, I think she would have loved you anyway.

I never saw her love for you falter or change, even when she got really sick and we had to move from California."

He just shook his head. "If that bitch hadn't fired me, we'd have managed. It's her fault your mom died the way she did. If I could only have stayed in my job and kept my benefits, your mom would still be alive today."

"We don't know that."

"I know that. And I want Alice Horvath and her sanctimonious family to pay for what they did to us. They deserve to be taught a lesson. They could've afforded a few hundred thousand here and there. There was no need for them to punish me the way they did. I need vengeance, Peyton. I deserve it. Your mother deserves it. You deserve it. I can't do it myself, so you have to do it for me. You have to!"

His eyes took on a haze of fury and Peyton realized it was very possible that he wasn't entirely sane. Maybe he never had been. He'd always been prone to irrational outbursts. And his love for her mother had bordered on obsessive; she could see that now. But his choices and actions, they were all on him, whether he could admit to them or not.

She felt as if the scales had been ripped from her eyes. All these years she'd believed him to be the innocent party, somehow unfairly wronged in the process that had seen him lose his job and their lifestyle. And now she knew the truth. He had stolen the money from Horvath Corporation. He had falsified reports. The knowledge that he'd been guilty all along, while proclaiming his innocence and acting the injured party, was devastating. All these years she'd been coached by her father to hate the Horvath family, when all along they'd been innocent. The very people she'd been brought up to vilify, the people who'd welcomed her into their family with open arms, had been the victims all along.

"I'm not doing it, Dad."

"You have to," he repeated.

"No, I don't. It's time to let go of your anger, if you can. You know you did wrong and I'm grateful you've finally told me the truth."

"The truth is they deserve everything they get. They need to be knocked down a peg or two."

"No, Dad, they don't." Something Alice had said to her last night about protecting her and her mom tickled at the back of her mind. "They could have pressed criminal charges against you back then, do you realize that? Alice Horvath chose to only fire you because she knew if she pressed charges that Mom and I would suffer even more."

"She should have let me keep my job." He remained adamant.

"Would you have done that in the same position?"

"I always meant to give the money back," he said sullenly.

"I'm sure you did," Peyton answered sadly. "Dad?"

"What now?"

"I have a daughter."

"That child Galen Horvath is looking after?"

"Yes. She's my daughter."

Finally, something in her tone made her father look at her and meet her eyes. "The baby you gave away?"

"Yes."

"More meddling from that bitch, I suppose."

"No, more *care* from Alice Horvath. She made it possible for me to finish college, Dad, without loans. She made sure my baby went to a loving home with people who cared for her as if she was their own. And when they died suddenly, she gave me a second chance at motherhood."

Magnus looked away from her and toward his surf rod, noting it was bucking away with a fish on the line.

"I've got to go," he said.

"Dad? Don't you want to see her? My daughter? Your granddaughter?"

He shook his head. "No. I want to be left alone."

If he'd taken his filleting knife out and sliced her heart from her chest he couldn't have done any more harm than he'd done with his words right now. Choking back the tears that threatened to fall, she nodded in response.

"Fine, I'll go. I love you, Dad."

No response. She turned and walked down the beach toward the stairs that led up the bluff to her car, unaware of the wind that tugged at her hair, whipping it across her face until she could barely see. She shouldn't have expected any different, she told herself. He'd always been this way. But not to even want to see a picture of his own granddaughter? That was a blow she hadn't been expecting.

As she drove the two-and-a-half-hour journey back to the airport in Portland she mulled over the exchange with her dad. It had gone exactly as she'd expected, even if it hadn't gone as she'd hoped. But he'd finally told her the truth about what he'd done and, in doing so, had rendered her fight with the Horvaths to be null and void. She had no bone to pick with them. Her article, as Alice had so rightly pointed out last night, had been slanted by her father's twisted version of events and was now not even worth the kilobytes of space it took up on her hard drive.

After her flight from Portland to SeaTac, she headed to the parking garage. Before starting her car, she took her laptop and a clean USB drive from her bag and transferred the article she'd written to the drive before wiping it from her computer hard drive and from her cloud storage. Then she drove the two-hour journey home.

By the time she pulled up in front of the house it was dark and she was absolutely shattered. But there was one last thing she had to do today. Despite the late hour, Alice responded to her knock on the guest suite door looking composed and elegant with a string of lustrous pearls around her lined neck, her makeup perfect and not a hair out of place.

"Peyton? Are you all right, my dear? You look worn out. Come in."

"No, I won't come in. This won't take long." Peyton drew in a deep breath and began to talk. "I...I wanted to apologize for what I've done. I was wrong and I...I have something for you." Peyton held the USB drive out to Alice, who took it automatically. "It's the article. The only copy. It's up to you what happens to it."

"Ah," Alice uttered, her tone filled with a wealth of understanding. "I see. You've been to see your father today?"

Peyton nodded.

"Then," Alice continued, "I think you should have this back. You will do with it what is right. And, Peyton?"

"Yes?"

Alice frowned for a moment before shaking her head briefly. "No, it's not my place to say anything. I've said and done enough. Sometimes life puts us on a path we didn't mean to take, but only we can make the decision to take a new course or to attempt to forge on the way we're going. Just trust your heart, my dear, and you won't go wrong."

Nineteen

Ellie had long since gone to bed and Peyton assumed Galen was watching TV upstairs in the lounge off the master bedroom. She went up to her office, closed the door and set her laptop on the desk and started to write.

The sun was rising as she finished proofreading what she'd written. Finally satisfied, she attached the file to an email to her editor and pressed Send. There, it was done. Whatever happened next was out of her control.

She could hear Ellie stirring as she passed the girl's bedroom, so she knocked gently on the door.

"Good morning," she said as a sleepy face with tousled hair popped out from the covers. *Her daughter*, she thought with a sharp tug at her heart. She fought to keep her voice even. "Sleep well?"

"Yes. I missed you last night, though."

"You were already asleep when I got back."

"Are you wearing the same clothes you wore yesterday?" Ellie asked.

"Yeah. I haven't been to bed yet. There was something I had to finish. Now it's done."

"Was it really important?"

Peyton nodded. "I'm going to catch a few hours' sleep now, but I'll see you after school, okay?"

"Okay. Sweet dreams, Mom."

Peyton felt her heart shudder in her chest. Mom? Had that been a slip of the tongue, or had Ellie begun to truly see Peyton as her mother? She wanted with all her heart to rush into Ellie's room, scoop her into her arms and hold her as tight as she could, but she forced herself to blow a kiss instead and close Ellie's door behind her.

She turned around and came to an abrupt halt when she realized Galen was standing on the landing, waiting for her. As tired as she was, Peyton couldn't control the swell of desire that rippled through her body at the sight of him. Fresh from the shower, his hair wet but combed, his suit and shirt crisp and clean, he was the personification of the successful businessman. But she knew that beneath the layers of his corporate attire was a complex man with complex needs and desires that equaled her own. How was she ever going to bridge this distance that she'd created between them? Would he ever trust her again?

"So? Did you speak to him?" His tone was not in the least welcoming or friendly.

"I did. And I've apologized to your grandmother. Now I want to apologize to you."

Behind her, Ellie sprang from her bedroom. "Last one down to breakfast is a rotten egg!"

She danced away down the stairs and Galen's eyes followed her. Peyton looked at him, drinking him in, wondering if this would be one of her last chances to do so.

"We need to talk," he said abruptly. "But not now. This evening."

She nodded and watched as he went down the stairs after Ellie, before stumbling to her room and falling into her bed fully clothed.

Peyton slept heavily, only waking when she heard the front door slam to announce Ellie's arrival home from school. She shoved her hair out of her face and looked at the clock for confirmation. She hadn't meant to sleep this late—she'd even missed saying good-bye to Alice, who had flown home at lunchtime. She shucked off her clothes and dived into the shower, thankful that they had Maggie to welcome Ellie home and see to her post-school day needs. There were some distinct advantages to wealth on the scale that the Horvath family enjoyed, she forced herself to admit.

She spent the afternoon with Ellie, marking time until Galen was home from work and they could have that talk. By the time Ellie had gone to bed, he still wasn't home and Peyton's stomach was tied up in knots. She couldn't settle—alternately pacing the downstairs sitting room floor, or opening the refrigerator door for something to eat even though she couldn't bear the thought of food in her stomach. It was close to ten o'clock when she heard the front door open.

Peyton walked to the main entrance and stopped in her tracks as she saw Galen standing there. He looked exhausted. Every cell in her body urged her to welcome him home, to comfort him—but she'd lost that right, and the realization tore through her with a visceral pain.

"Thanks for waiting," he said. "I have a lot I need to say to you. I'll just go put my case in my office and I'll meet you in the den, okay?"

The den, not the sitting room? It was cozier in there. Was that a sign that this discussion was going to be kinder than she deserved? She didn't know how she'd handle kind. She certainly didn't deserve it. She went to the bar and poured a couple of brandies and went to wait.

She didn't have to wait long. Peyton handed Galen his drink, momentarily basking in the thrill of her fingers brushing against his as he took the glass from her.

"Before you say anything," she said, determined to preempt him, "I want to apologize for my actions in using Match Made in Marriage and, in particular, marrying you to further my own agenda. I shouldn't have been so cavalier with you or with Ellie and I'm deeply ashamed that I was. I went to see my father yesterday and I learned some painful, eye-opening truths. They made me realize exactly what I've done here, to you and to Ellie. Made me realize, too, that somewhere along the line I'd become as harmful and toxic as my father. I didn't like having that mirror held up to me. So—" she sucked in a deep breath and rushed the words she'd been practicing all evening "—I'm leaving. I have a new assignment coming up and there's no point in me staying here when we both know we can't go on. I won't contest a divorce. In fact, I'll begin proceedings if that's what you prefer. And Ellie..."

Peyton blinked hard against the burning sensation in her eyes. "I won't fight you for custody of Ellie. You were right. I gave her up before, I made my choice then, and I have no right to change my mind now that I've been fortunate enough to find her again. I have no right to usurp what you two have together, what her *parents* wanted for her. I don't want to unsettle her when she's already been through so much. With your agreement, however, I would like visitation rights, to see her and get to watch her grow up—" Her throat dried up completely, making further speech impossible.

She took a sip of her drink, letting the brandy burn a path down her throat to the pit of her churning stomach. Galen hadn't said a word. He just sat there, watching her, his expression inscrutable.

"I've already packed and loaded my car. I can't face saying goodbye to Ellie again, so please don't expect it of me. In fact, it's hard enough to say goodbye to you. We had some good times, didn't we?"

Galen looked pained. "Is this really what you want? To just walk out and pretend we never happened?"

She nodded, her eyes awash with tears. "Please don't say anything. I just... I...have to go."

Peyton carefully put her glass down on the coffee table between them and stood. "Thank you again for everything you've tried to do for me. And thank you for looking after Ellie. She's so lucky to have you. I...I hope that one day you find a woman who can give you the family you and Ellie deserve."

And with that, Peyton fled from the room and down the passageway. She heard Galen's voice behind her but she didn't dare stop or look around. She went straight for the front door, down the main steps and into her car. She struggled to put the key in the ignition and saw Galen's form loom in the front door just as she managed to insert the key and turn it. Her car fired to life and she put it into gear and pressed on the accelerator. And then she was on her way— her child, the man she loved and all her unspoken dreams left behind.

Galen stood at the entrance to the apartment and checked the address he'd been given, then knocked firmly at the door. He heard sounds from inside, then the scrape of a chain on the door and the turn of a lock. The door opened a few inches and he caught his first glimpse of Peyton's face in three endless weeks.

"I've read your article," he stated. "Can I come in?"

"What? How? It's not even in print yet." She narrowed her eyes.

"It wasn't what I was expecting."

"I'm assuming you had some kind of injunction on my work?"

"I did, and I make no apology for that. I protect what's mine. Peyton, let me in."

"Ever heard of freedom of the press?"

"I was especially impressed how you showed that even through her grief over my grandfather's death, and the subsequent deaths of my father and my uncle from the same heart condition, she kept a firm hand on the running of the business. And how she maintained her leadership of the corporation with compassion and a fair hand. It was far more than I expected. No lies. You did good work."

"Damned with faint praise," she muttered, but she closed the door a little and he listened as she slid the chain off. "What do you want?"

"To talk. You left without hearing me out."

"That was three weeks ago," she pointed out, her tone bitter.

He let his gaze roam over her. She'd lost weight she could ill afford to lose in the past three weeks.

"Peyton, let me inside. I'm not having this discussion on your doorstep."

"Fine," she said. "Come in, then."

"I took the time to think about what you said that night. About you leaving us. And—" he reached into his suit pocket to withdraw the petition to dissolve their marriage "—I received this."

"I'm glad to see my lawyers are worth their exorbitant fee."

He looked around the apartment. Spartan with the

bare minimum of furnishings. The only thing that he saw that contained an ounce of her personality was a framed picture of her and Ellie on the beach in Hawaii. He remembered that day vividly and remembered taking that photo. He realized that it was probably at that point that he'd begun to fall in love with her. How had he not seen the similarities between her and Ellie then? They were like peas in a pod with their sandy-brown, sun-kissed hair, the tilt of their noses, the clarity in their gray-blue eyes. For that moment in time they'd been happy, a family.

"Nice place," he commented.

"Don't lie, Galen. What do you want from me?"

"I wanted to know why you changed the article."

"I told you the night I left. I found out the truth from my father. I couldn't send the article as it was anymore. Alice deserved better. You all did."

"Why didn't you tell me you had changed it?"

She shrugged. "I didn't think it would change anything between us. I'm sorry, Galen. When I researched and wrote the original piece, I believed that what I'd been told was the truth. In fact, growing up, it was *my* truth. It was all I ever heard from my father, and I saw nothing that made me believe any differently... until I met you."

"And now?"

"Now I'm back where I was at the beginning. Alone, but wiser." She gestured to the divorce papers. "Have you come to bring these back? You could have used a courier. You've signed them?"

"I haven't. And I'm not going to."

"What? Why not?"

"Because I want you back. Come home."

"What?"

"Come home. I want you back. In my life, in our marriage, in my bed. Ellie wants you back, too. She misses you and she has every right to understand that you're her birth mother. She needs you in her life."

"I asked if I could see her sometimes—"

"No. Not sometimes. She deserves better than that. You both do. We all do. Come home. You say you changed the article because you learned the truth, but you never stopped to discover the rest of the truth about us. I love you, Peyton, even with all your prickles and barbs and the walls you constantly keep trying to raise between us—and I believe you love me, too. I'm happy to wait for when you're ready to admit it. I can wait until my dying day if I have to, but I cannot wait another moment to have you back in my life. Unless, of course, you can convince me you don't love me, or *can't* love me. If that's the case, then I'll turn around and walk out your door, but I believe that somewhere in our crazy, mixed-up marriage we both did something right, that we found something together that we can build on and grow to last a lifetime.

"Please, Peyton, say you'll come home to us. To me."

"I don't know, Galen. I'm terrified to give in to love. I saw what it did to my father. How his love for my mom drove him to do stupid things like stealing and lying. He's a broken man. He didn't even want to see a photo of Ellie when I went to see him. How can I be what she needs when I don't even know how to be a good parent?

"All these years, ever since I gave her up for adoption, I've strived not to love, not to let go of my control over my life. Being with you and Ellie was tough at first because I kept fighting my feelings for both of you. But then I started to relax. I let go of those reins and I allowed myself to begin to love Ellie. Finding out she was really my daughter was terrifying to me, while being the greatest gift of my life at the same time. I wanted to grab her and run, but I knew I couldn't do that—to her or to you. I knew being with you had started to strip away the barriers and safeguards that I had built up ever since childhood. It frightened me."

She took a deep breath and then looked directly into his eyes. "I love you, Galen. I didn't want to. I fought against it. I even used sex to try and distract myself from it."

"Well, you can feel free to distract yourself anytime you want to. Just saying."

She laughed at his attempt to lighten the seriousness of the moment. It was a sound of pure joy.

"Thanks," she said when she got her laughter under control. "I'll take that under consideration."

"So you're okay if I do this?" He held the divorce papers in front of him and tore them in half.

"Yeah, I'm okay if you do that."

Galen tossed the scraps onto a nearby chair. "And you're okay if I do this?"

He stepped closer, took her in his arms, bent his

head and took her lips with his. She remained still for a split second, making him wonder if he'd taken a step too far, too soon, but then she softened in his arms, her mouth responding beneath his. Their lips meshing, tongues grazing. He forced himself to pull back, to allow her to make the next move, and prayed that it would be the right one for them both.

"I'm very okay if you do that," she answered breathlessly. "In fact, I'm okay if you do that again, just to be sure."

Ever a gentleman, Galen did, and when he broke off the embrace he looked deeply into her eyes.

"Peyton, will you come home with me? Will you be my wife in every sense? Be Ellie's mom? Be our lives?"

"I will. These past few weeks have been hell. I can't seem to function without you and I don't want to anymore."

He allowed himself a smile. His proud, fiercely independent wife had just admitted more than she probably realized. "Then let's go home."

"Yes, I'd like that. For good this time."

"Forever."

* * * * *

COMING NEXT MONTH FROM

Available May 7, 2019

#2659 THAT NIGHT IN TEXAS
Texas Cattleman's Club: Houston • by Joss Wood
When an accident sends Vivian Donner to the hospital, Camden McNeal is shocked to find out he's her emergency contact—and the father of her child. As floodwaters rise, he brings his surprise family home, but will their desire last through a storm of secrets?

#2660 MARRIAGE AT ANY PRICE
The Masters of Texas • by Lauren Canan
Seth Masters needs a wife. Ally Kincaid wants her ranch back after his family's company took it from her. It's a paper marriage made in mutual distrust...and far too much sizzling attraction for it to end conveniently!

#2661 TEXAN FOR THE TAKING
Boone Brothers of Texas • by Charlene Sands
Drea McDonald is determined to honor her mother's memory even though it means working with Mason Boone, who was the first man to break her heart. But as old passions flare, can she resist the devil she knows?

#2662 TEMPTED BY SCANDAL
Dynasties: Secrets of the A-List • by Karen Booth
Matt Richmond is the perfect man for Nadia Gonzalez, except for one slight hitch—he's her boss! But when their passion is too strong to resist, it isn't long before a mysterious someone threatens to destroy everything she's worked for...

#2663 A CONTRACT SEDUCTION
Southern Secrets • by Janice Maynard
Jonathan Tarleton needs to marry Lisette to save his company. She's the only one he trusts. But in return, she wants one thing—a baby. With time running out, can their contract marriage survive their passion...and lead to an unexpected chance at love?

#2664 WANTED: BILLIONAIRE'S WIFE
by Susannah Erwin
When a major deal goes wrong, businessman Luke Dallas needs to hire a temporary wife. Danica Novak, an executive recruiter, agrees to play unconventional matchmaker—for the right price. But when no one measures up, is it because the perfect woman was at his side all along?

**YOU CAN FIND MORE INFORMATION ON UPCOMING HARLEQUIN® TITLES,
FREE EXCERPTS AND MORE AT WWW.HARLEQUIN.COM.**

HDCNM0419

Get 4 FREE REWARDS!

We'll send you 2 FREE Books plus 2 FREE Mystery Gifts.

Harlequin® Desire books feature heroes who have it all: wealth, status, incredible good looks... everything but the right woman.

FREE Value Over $20

SPECIAL EXCERPT FROM

Read on for a sneak peek at the new book in
New York Times *bestselling author Lori Foster's*
sizzling Road to Love series, Slow Ride*!*

"You live in a secluded paradise." Rain started, a light sprinkling that grew stronger in seconds until it lashed the car windows. The interior immediately fogged—probably from her accelerated breathing.

Jack smiled. "There are other houses." The wipers added a rhythmic thrum to the sound of the rainfall. "The mature trees make it seem more remote than it is." Rather than take the driveway to the front of the house, he pulled around back to a carport. "The garage is filled with tools, so Brodie helped me put up a shelter as a temporary place to park."

Ronnie was too busy removing her seat belt and looking at the incredible surroundings to pay much attention to where he parked—until he turned off the engine. Then the intoxicating feel of his attention enveloped her.

Her gaze shot to his. *Think of your future*, she told herself. *Think of how he'll screw up the job if he sticks around.*

He'd half turned to face her, one forearm draped over the wheel. After his gaze traced every feature of her face with almost tactile concentration, he murmured, "We'll wait here just a minute to see if the storm blows over."

Here, in this small space? With only a console, their warm breath and hunger between them?

Did the man think she was made of stone?

She swallowed heavily, already tempted beyond measure. A boom of thunder resonated in her chest, and she barely noticed, not with her gaze locked on his and the tension ramping up with every heartbeat.

Suddenly she knew. No matter what happened with the job, regardless of how he might irk her, she'd never again experience sexual chemistry this strong and she'd be a fool not to explore it.

She'd like to think she wasn't a fool.

"Jack…" The word emerged as a barely there whisper, a question, an admission. Yearning.

As if he understood, he shifted toward her, his eyes gone darker with intent. "One kiss, Ronnie. I need that."

God, she needed it more. Anticipation sizzling, heart swelling, she met him halfway over the console.

His mouth grazed her cheek so very softly, leaving a trail of heat along her jaw, her chin. "You have incredible skin."

Skin? Who cared about her skin? "Kiss me."

"Yes, ma'am." As his lips finally met hers in a bold, firm press, his hand, so incredibly large, cupped the base of her skull and angled her for a perfect fit.

Ronnie was instantly lost.

She didn't recall reaching for him, but suddenly her fingers were buried in his hair and she somehow hung over the center console.

They were no longer poised between the seats, two mouths meeting in neutral ground. She pressed him back in his seat as she took the kiss she wanted, the kiss she needed.

Whether she opened her mouth to invite his tongue, or his tongue forged the way, she didn't know and honestly didn't care, not with the heady taste of him making her want more, more, *more*.

Don't miss Lori Foster's Slow Ride,
available soon from HQN Books!